"I can't say that I'm glad I'm stuck in Montana, but something good has come out of this."

"Maybe after you have fun with us and get in your social time, you'll change your mind about Montana?" Luke said.

"I'm not sure it can be done," Honor quipped. "But I'm liking the chance to actually make new friends."

"Good. I'm going to change your mind."

"Is that a warning or a threat?"

"Depends on which one will work."

"Neither." She tipped back her head and laughed. "I'm not going to change my mind. I'm a California girl. I miss the beach."

"We've got riverbanks."

"So not the same."

They laughed together. He liked Honor as much in real life as he had online. As he watched her walk away, his throat tightened, making it hard to swallow. A swirl of her blue dress's hem, a clip of her fancy shoes and a flip of her sleek honey hair and he was hooked just a little bit more.

It's never going to happen, he told himself. Did that stop him from liking her more?

Not a chance.

Books by Jillian Hart

JILLIAN HART

grew up on her family's homestead, where she helped raise cattle, rode horses and scribbled stories in her spare time. After earning her English degree from Whitman College, she worked in travel and advertising before selling her first novel. When Jillian isn't working on her next story, she can be found puttering in her rose garden, curled up with a good book or spending quiet evenings at home with her family.

JILLIAN HART

Montana Cowboy

Love Inspired

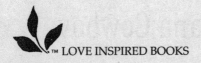

™ LOVE INSPIRED BOOKS

Recycling programs for this product may not exist in your area.

ISBN-13: 978-0-373-87751-5

MONTANA COWBOY

www.LoveInspiredBooks.com

Printed in U.S.A.

Direct my steps by your word.
—*Psalms* 119:133

Chapter One

"My life stinks."

Honor Crosby could sympathize with the teenage boy trudging ahead of her through the woods. Some bug swooped at her. She batted it out of her face and ignored the flutter of something high up in the trees and tried not to think of what might be lurking overhead. A giant mosquito, a gross spider, who knew? And worse, her poor shoes. They were sinking in the squishy carpet of dead pine needles and moss, an aspen leaf skewered on one heel.

"Sure, but you don't have to make life harder than it has to be," she told the kid with his hangdog expression. "You waste more time trying to put off your work than actually doing it. If you jumped in and got your studying over with, you'd have more free time."

"I don't want to study at all. It's summer. I don't need to get into that stupid school and I don't need a tutor." He hung his head. Jerrod Lambert wasn't a bad kid—not at all. Just an unhappy one.

Understanding filled her as she remembered being a teenager trying to handle her parents' pressure to succeed. She knew where Jerrod was coming from, but the

Lord was a great comfort and she prayed Jerrod would lean on his faith more to find solutions to his problems instead of running away from them.

"I'm not so bad of a tutor, am I?" she asked.

"Much better than the last one, but that's not the point." Jerrod blew out a sigh as he tromped through the underbrush and broke out into the bright sunshine. "I'd rather be dirt biking."

"And I'd rather be at the beach club with an icy soda in one hand and my e-reader in the other." For an instant, the remembered roar of the ocean, the sweep of the waves on the sandy shore and the chime of cheerful conversation felt so real she could almost feel herself there, where she belonged.

She missed home and her posse of friends so much she almost stumbled when her heels hit the manicured lawn. Leaving home had been an impulsive decision and not the most brilliant one she'd ever made. Montana, she mused as she pulled the leaf off her shoe heel. What had she been thinking?

"Honor?"

"What, kiddo?"

"What is it like at Wheatly?"

"It's one of the best Christian schools in southern California." She'd gone there as a teen and returned after college to teach English. She loved the school and the community of teachers and staff that felt more like family than coworkers. She missed them sorely, too. With the current economy, her job had been cut, since she'd been the newest teacher there. Her dearest wish was to return to her beloved Wheatly and teach once again. Maybe when the economy improved? A girl could hope. "I hated leaving. Actually, I didn't really leave. I substituted there for most of last year."

"And then I came along, needing tutoring."

"Once you're there, you'll love it. I promise." She tromped up the stone steps, ignoring the rugged scenery and architecture that surrounded her—high mountain peaks, stone masonry and a sprawling log-and-glass estate that simply could not compare to Malibu. Nothing on earth could.

"If I pass the test, that is. You sound like my dad." Not encouraged, Jerrod's head hung lower looking like a prisoner on his way to death row, dragging his feet across the deck. "I won't tell if we don't work this afternoon. My dad would never know."

"But I would." She opened a glass-framed door. "In you go. It won't be so bad, I promise."

"Yeah, I've heard that before." Unconvinced, he plodded into the air-conditioned library and slung himself into an overstuffed chair. "I'd rather be dirt biking."

"Who wouldn't?" Honor quipped, not quite able to relate. She was no outdoors girl...unless hanging poolside counted. She plucked a book off the Chippendale writing desk and handed it to the bummed teenager. "Start reading, kid. Think of it this way, if you ace the entrance exam on the first try, then you won't ever have to deal with another tutor."

"You're not seeing the problem." Jerrod blew out a sigh. "I'm wasting my summer in here."

"I get it." She slipped into the upholstered chair behind the desk, where her laptop sat. "Sorry, but you still have to read the book."

Another beleaguered sigh and the tome opened, the teenager bowed his head and at least it looked as though he were reading.

She knew exactly how Jerrod felt. This was her summer, too. She hadn't planned to spend most of it being a private tutor, but at the time it seemed like a brilliant option to get away from a certain man. Little did she realize she would be hidden away at the Lambert family compound in the middle of the wilderness. Literally. Forests stretched in every direction and the nearest town was forty minutes away.

Which meant email was her best link to civilization. Since her student was busy and she'd caught up on all her work, she turned to her laptop. Her best friend and roommate's message filled the screen.

Totally missing you! Kelsey wrote. We're off to the movies. Wish you were here!

Me, too, she thought with a pang. Onto the next email.

We're sitting in the theater, read Anna Louise's message, sent from her phone. Kelsey had to go and buy the jumbo popcorn. Can't stop eating it. Miss you!

Yeah, she could almost taste that popcorn. She gave a little sigh, glanced out the wall of windows overlooking a shocking amount of trees. *Just three more weeks,* she told herself. *Jerrod will take his exams, my job here will be done and I'm back home.*

She went on to her next email.

Honor, we missed you at the book chat last night, Luke's message read. Where were you?

Luke McKaslin. Her online buddy—well, she didn't know what other word to use to describe him. She gave a little sigh of exasperation, or was it confusion? She didn't know which.

When she'd arrived here in March, stuck in the middle of nowhere, she'd gone into serious withdrawal, so she went looking for social connections online. She'd kept up with her friends and joined Good Books, a social network and a site devoted to books.

That was where she met Luke, or Montana Cowboy as he was known on the book site. She'd made a lot of online friends on the site, and Luke was one of them. Okay, a special one of them. They'd just hit it off right from the start.

Mrs. Lambert had a big barbecue, she typed. I meant to get away and sneak onto my computer, but I had a surprisingly good time. I miss being social, so I couldn't make myself break away. How did the book discussion go?

She hit Send. One of her great loves in life was books. She loved reading. Always had, always would. Maybe that's what she liked about Luke best. He felt the same way.

A beleaguered sigh drew her attention.

"Are you really reading that book or just staring at the same page?" she asked Jerrod. "Maybe you're napping?"

"Sorry." He shook his head and at least made the appearance of making an effort to read.

Funny kid. She squinted at her screen, smiling to see Luke's next email. He must be sitting at his computer, too.

The discussion wasn't as lively without you, he wrote. Still missing home?

You know it, she tapped out. I know you like living in Montana, but how do you do it?

I've always lived here, came his reply. So it's hard to say since I don't have much to compare it to. I read a lot. I ride my horse. I hang with the cows.

That's about what I expect from a cowboy. Honestly. If she wasn't a California girl and she wasn't not looking for a boyfriend—and she so, so wasn't—then

Luke's gentle humor would be just the thing to spark her interest.

If. That was a very big if. Thinking of Kip, she shook her head. Yep, she was off the market. For a long, long time.

There aren't any cows or horses here, not that I would know what to do with them. I never hit that horse crazy phase a few of my friends went through.

I've never left mine, he answered. But if you're missing hanging with people...

You mean instead of trees? She typed, biting back her smile.

My sister is getting married tomorrow. I know it's last minute, but Bozeman is only a few hours' drive for you—

A few hours' drive was considered not a big deal in Montana. That always cracked her up.

—but it will be fun, you'll get in some social time and I think you'll like my sisters.

I'm sure they're nice. But that didn't mean she should meet some man she didn't know, at least face-to-face. Online he was nice and she felt safe chatting with him. He was respectful and funny and friendly. But in person? Who knew what he could be like? Hadn't she believed in the man Kip pretended to be?

You couldn't always tell who someone was behind the mask they wore.

I get it, if you don't want to come. It's your day off. You might not want to spend four hours of it in the car.

Yes, that's true. And it was. She didn't want to drive that far, but wouldn't it be fun to meet him? He'd always come across as an amiable guy. Not overly ambitious, and decent in a country boy sort of way. She'd absolutely looked up his profile on the website when she first "met" him. His picture had been friendly—really great smile, honest violet-blue eyes and talk about handsome. At thirty, he was five years older than her, and he was solid.

She'd liked that.

"Jerrod, are you asleep?"

"Whaa?" His head snapped up. He looked around and picked up the book he dropped. "Sorry."

This wasn't the first time she feared that kid wasn't going to pass the entrance exam. But at least she wouldn't be stuck in this isolated—but lovely—spot the rest of the summer. Three more weeks and she would be in her car driving toward the state line. Woo-hoo! She couldn't wait.

Luke's email popped on her screen. Too bad you can't come. You'll be missing out on some pretty good cake.

Cake? Why didn't you say so? Now I'm really tempted. Plus, I could get out of this house. Didn't a change of scenery sound like just the thing? She was tempted to accept. She had fun chatting with him online. Would it be even more fun in person? She did miss having friends and going places. Maybe she would say yes—

A knock rapped on the door. Mrs. Lambert sashayed in. She was tall, lean and eternally youthful thanks to a good dermatologist and Botox injections. "Honor? May I have a word with you?"

"Yes." She gave thanks that Jerrod's nose was studiously in his book—or at least it appeared that way—as she rose from the desk. She tapped into the hallway.

"I saw you and Jerrod. Coming in from the forest." Olive Lambert drew herself up. "He ran off again, didn't he? And you didn't inform me."

"It was just for a few moments. He didn't go far."

"How many times do I have to tell you? He's fifteen. He's old enough to learn the value of self-discipline. If he can't do it for himself, then you will do it for him." Concern softened harsh words, but not enough. Olive Lambert was a woman used to setting the standards and getting her own way.

In the library, Jerrod's head bowed lower. Honor couldn't see his face, just the tense corner of his jaw. The poor kid. "He's doing well over all. You know he is. He's worked hard all week."

"When he wasn't trying to sneak off to ride his bike," Olive interrupted. "You need to keep a better eye on him. Let's try a little harder, shall we?"

A movement out of the corner of her eye caught her attention. Jerrod's head bobbed lower, his total misery palpable.

It hadn't been an easy time for the Lambert family, with their impending divorce. She'd watched the fall-out when her parent's marriage failed, so she understood. She wished she knew how to make it easier for her student.

"Of course." She watched Olive tap down the wide corridor, heel strikes knelling on imported marble.

Well, that could have gone better.

Inside the library came the thud of a book slamming shut in frustration. Jerrod stayed in his chair, firsts clenched, muscles bunched in his jaw, upset.

Lord, please help me find a way to help him. He was a good kid.

"I didn't mean to get you into trouble," he muttered, resigned. "I just wanted to get out of this house."

"I know. You've been studying so hard."

"I don't want to fail it again. It's embarrassing taking the makeup exam as it is." With a frustrated sigh, he opened his book. "I'm tired of being stuck here. There's hardly anything to do. I wish—"

He didn't finish that thought. Instead, he launched out of his chair with his book in hand. "I'm going outside."

"Okay, but—"

"I really need to get this book read. I know, I know." Jerrod rolled his eyes and shouldered open the door.

Funny kid. When she glanced at her screen, a picture of a gorgeous wedding cake—three beautifully decorated tiers—stared at her, a picture embedded in Luke's email.

Chocolate, chocolate chip cake, he wrote. Cream cheese frosting. Lots of icing flowers, as you can see. Voted by all four of my sisters as the best-tasting cake in existence. Tempted?

Very, she wrote, hesitating. Luke was nice. He was friendly and funny and kind-hearted in his comments on the website and in the messages they had been sending back and forth over the last few months. She'd had fun corresponding with him. Maybe it would be fun to meet him?

Then again, maybe she'd regret it. Luke McKaslin could be too good to be true. She clicked her way to the Good Books site and his user profile. His picture was a casual shot of a muscular, lean man sitting on a front porch step with one arm slung around his black border collie.

A Stetson shaded his strong, chiseled face. His bright violet-blue eyes radiated honesty and good humor. His high cheekbones, perfect sloping nose and square jaw could have been carved out of granite and were softened by the wide generous curve of his smile.

A big-hearted smile, she decided. Wide, approachable, a totally-good-guy kind of smile.

The fact that he was completely gorgeous didn't enter into the equation. She wasn't looking for gorgeous. She wasn't looking at all. Period. She was taking a break from romance. Unequivocally.

But friendship? Yes, that was something she could definitely do. Luke McKaslin and his amiable, country-strong qualities made her want to drive two hours just to meet him.

She stared at his info at the end of his message. A video chat? Sure, why not.

"Honor?" Luke's handsome face filled her screen— iron features, vivid, almost-purple eyes and yet it was his warmth that struck her most. "Hey, it's good to actually talk at you instead of type."

"It's weird, isn't it?" He was a perfect stranger, and yet he wasn't. She thought of all the notes they'd written back and forth about books and, lately, about life. She knew he lived on a ranch northeast of Bozeman. His dog's name was Nell. His younger brother had died years ago fighting forest fires. He ran a dairy with his older brother. "I feel as if I should be typing something."

"Me, too. This is new, talking instead of typing, but it's nice. You look different from your profile picture."

"I do?"

"Blonder. More serious."

"It's because of summer," she explained, since the sun tended to lighten her hair. "And Montana."

"You're still not liking Montana?" He nodded, scattering light brown hair with sun-made highlights. "It's a beautiful place to visit, but it is different living here. I thought you might get used to it by now."

"I'm still counting the days until I leave. I miss home."

"Sure, I get that. It's not just where you are, it's who you're with."

"So, you really are like all those emails you've written."

"Yep. Nell didn't sneak onto the computer and do it for me. Right, girl?"

A bark rose in the background, echoing in what appeared to be an eating area off the kitchen. She could just see the edge of kitchen cabinets. A dog's nails tapped on linoleum. "Nell wants to know if you're really coming. Brooke's wedding should be a lot of fun."

"Most weddings are a happy event, but a lot of fun? Not so much." She thought of her sister's recent wedding, with all the stress, the preparations and pressure.

"That's because you haven't been to a McKaslin family wedding." Twinkles sparkled in his eyes. Amiable, good-humored and decent, that's how Luke came across to her. He raked one hand through his thick hair. "We know how to have a good time. You wouldn't happen to be hiding any champion volleyball skills, would you?"

"I play on my church team. Or I used to, before I moved here."

"Okay, now you have to come. Because Brooke is a whiz at volleyball and she thinks she has tomorrow's game won hands down."

"Volleyball at a wedding reception?"

"Now you think I'm hokey and you wouldn't get near me with a ten-foot pole." Dimples tucked into the corners of his generous smile.

A perfect smile. Good thing she wasn't interested or she might be a little dazzled. "I make no judgments," she reassured him. "You've just talked me into it."

"Yeah? Good." His smile broadened. His dimples dug a little deeper.

Wow. The impact was enough to knock her off her chair. She glanced over the top of her computer screen, totally forgetting her charge. Jerrod sat seemingly engrossed in his book on the porch. The poor kid needed a change of scenery, too. "Is it okay if I bring a guest?"

"Bring anyone you want. The more the merrier. I'm looking forward to meeting you in person, Honor."

"Me, too." She tried to ignore the dazzle of his dimples one more time. "You'll email me directions?"

"Absolutely. Whoops. That's my brother. It's milking time. I've got to head to the barn. The cows are waiting."

"Okay. Give Nell a pat for me."

"Will do." He leaned in, sincere. "Goodbye until tomorrow, Honor."

"Goodbye." She closed the lid of her laptop, realizing she was smiling. Really, truly smiling.

Montana might have a highlight, after all.

"Hey, Jerrod," she called. "How would you like an outing tomorrow?"

Chapter Two

"Is that Honor?" His sister, Colbie, elbowed Luke in the ribs, her quiet whisper startling him out of the minister's sermon.

Keeping one ear on the service, he glanced over his shoulder. A lean woman with sleek blond hair closed the church door carefully, making little noise as she took a step.

"That's her." He'd know her anywhere. Her heart-shaped face, her graceful movements and the openness in her big blue eyes as she scanned the sanctuary. His heart kicked when their gazes met.

A tentative smile touched her lips. Recognition roared through him so hard, he gripped the pew back for support. The lanky teenager who was with her led the way to the back row, where they quietly took a seat.

"She's really pretty." Colbie waggled her brows, her attention focused on the pulpit. "And she drove all that way. That's all I'm saying."

"She doesn't like me like that," he whispered in argument, knowing what his optimistic half sister was thinking. Honor was lonely, that was all, he wanted to make that clear, but this wasn't the time or the place. He tried to concentrate on the message, but the minister's words echoed in his head, which had strangely emptied the instant Honor Crosby had walked through the door.

Across the aisle his other half sister, Brandi, gave him two thumbs-up.

Yikes, he thought. *Couldn't a man invite a lonely lady to church without everyone leaping to conclusions?*

Fine, those conclusions may be right, but two months of chatting online at a book site and through email didn't make for anything more than a friendship. Just because he was a little sweet on her didn't mean she felt the same way. How many messages had she written where she mentioned being homesick? Tons. No, Honor Crosby wasn't sticking around. After her job was done, she would be jetting back to Malibu where she so obviously belonged.

"Let us pray," intoned Pastor Bill. Rustling filled the sanctuary as heads bowed and hands clasped.

"Love her shoes," Brooke whispered, his other sister leaned in, pressing against his other elbow.

"Did you see her handbag?" Brianna added.

"Shhh!" Lil, tucked in her wheelchair, gave them a withering look, reminding them this was the Lord's house. They all fell silent.

Colbie reached over to pat her mother's hand. They were a mishmash family these days, a combination of the remains of three families divorce and deceit had broken. Luke thought of his father, ground his teeth and added a prayer of his own. *Lord, please help Dad to stay away. Brooke deserves a happy, trouble-free day.*

Amen chorused through the sanctuary. Beside him, his sister the bride beamed as the first notes of the final hymn rang out. He couldn't concentrate the way he usually did because he kept listening for one voice, a voice he'd heard only once last night during their video chat. Her presence tugged at him like gravity and no matter what he did, it remained, a pull on his heart he couldn't stop or explain.

Finally. The last chorus. His tongue stumbled over the familiar words while his pulse galloped unsteadily. A few more moments and they would meet face-to-face. He'd be with her, in the same place, in person, and the prospect made his palms sweat. The woman who'd caught his attention with her funny remarks on Good Books. The woman who typed with him back and forth during a chat on a bestseller they'd both loved and it took more than an hour before either of them realized they were the only ones left in the chat room. It had ended and everyone else had left and they hadn't even noticed.

He hadn't noticed because he'd been smitten. Instantly. When he'd known nothing about her but her sense of humor and her opinion on a book. Her personality had shone through the words she'd typed, and he'd been interested. Not that he wanted her to know. It wouldn't be wise to get involved with a woman who wouldn't be sticking around and who, in no way, felt the same. How many times had she called him a friend?

He'd learned the hard way that was the hint women used when they liked you, but didn't see you as boyfriend material and never would.

"Luke?" Someone nudged him in the ribs. Colbie, this time, and laughter danced in her eyes. "Earth to Luke. Come back to the planet."

"I wonder what has his attention?" Brooke asked from his other side, laughing, already knowing the answer. "Or who?"

Couldn't a guy keep one little crush a secret? He

shook his head. This was the downside of a big family. Everyone was in your business. He did his best grimace. "For your information, I'm concentrating. I'm a very pious man. This is church, Colbie."

"Right." Laughter bubbled out of her. "Your scowl doesn't come close to scaring me."

"Not at all," Brooke agreed. "Hunter has a much better one."

"Thank you," came a gruff acknowledgement from the pew behind them. Older brother, Hunter, cracked a rare smile. "I'm proud of it. I do my best."

"It shows," Lil quipped from her chair. Multiple sclerosis may have slowed her body, but her spirit was as bright as ever. "That's why you don't have a single pretty lady coming to see you."

"She's coming for the wedding," he corrected for the tenth time that morning. "She's a friend. Nothing more."

"Sure, you don't want to put that kind of pressure on it." Middle-aged and with a sleek cap of dark hair, Lil was a substitute mom and a good one. "You just let it happen naturally."

"How many times?" he asked, raising his eyes to the ceiling. "Friend, not girlfriend."

"I certainly hope not," laughed a melodic alto as warm as a summer morning.

He'd know that voice anywhere. Honor. She swept up the aisle in a pretty summer dress, looking amazing. His crazy pulse lurched to a stop. He turned, not daring to breathe but her nearness stuck him, anyway, like a punch to the gut.

"I'm not ready for anything that serious. I'm a free bird these days." Honor's warm, flawless smile made it impossible not to like her. "Hi, Luke. This is Jerrod. Sorry we were late."

"No problem. You never know what is going to delay you on a Montana highway."

"That's the truth! We got behind this huge semi carrying the biggest concrete tube thing I've ever seen. It must have been for a water or irrigation system or something, but it went twenty-six miles an hour and was nearly impossible to pass."

"She's a California driver, too," the teenager added with an eye roll. "Fearless. She tried passing like six times. Good thing she decided against it or we'd be in a ditch."

"He spent the whole way giving me advice. We don't have big concrete tube things in L.A. At least not one I've met on the road." She stopped to take a breath, clearly nervous, too. "I was afraid we'd be late for the wedding. I bought a gift, but it's in the car. I didn't want to bring it in for the service."

"I told you it wouldn't matter," Jerrod added in a friendly way. He looked like a good kid.

"I know, but I was worried about all the crackling. You know, the wrapping paper? Luke knows because I told him that I tend to be a klutz."

"I think you exaggerate." After seeing her grace and charm, he didn't believe for one moment her funny stories she'd typed at him were true. "You've been misleading me all this time, haven't you?"

"Me, mislead you? No way. I've been totally honest." She hesitated, bit her bottom lip and rolled her eyes heavenward, perhaps aware God was watching her especially close in church. "Uh, I've been mostly really honest," she corrected.

Making them all laugh. Making him like her more.

"I'm Colbie," his sister spoke up, apparently eager to start the introductions.

Sure, he thought, nodding. Easy to read the hope on his sister's faces. He stepped up, finishing the introductions. "Meet the twins, Brianna and Brandilyn."

"Hi," Bree and Brandi chorused identically.

"My brother, Hunter. And Brooke, the bride."

"Good to meet you, Honor." Brooke was the only one in the group who knew about his correspondence with Honor and, he suspected, understood his feelings about her. Brooke gave a toss of her dark hair, smiled and grabbed the arm of the man beside her. "This is Liam, who is about to become my husband in thirty minutes."

"And you're not even dressed yet." Honor looked concerned. "Do you need help? I come with experience. I've pitched in at all my sisters' weddings."

"I'll take you up on that." Brooke nodded, looking as if she liked Honor very much.

In fact, all his family did. Not hard to figure why. They had hopes for him—marital hopes—except for Hunter who stood in the back, practicing his scowl.

"You'd best come with us, dear." Lil reached out her hand.

"I saved the best for last." Luke cleared his throat. "Lil is a gem."

"So I see. So good to meet you." Honor took Lil's hand with a warm squeeze as she addressed the woman in the wheelchair. "Luke has told me about you all, but especially you, Lil. It's easy to see why he has such a soft spot for you."

Lil beamed at the compliment. "He's the special one. Luke is always there when we need him."

"That doesn't surprise me at all." She shot a glance at the tall, sandy-haired man blushing a little from the compliment.

"She exaggerates," he confessed.

"So I see." Now she had something else to like about Luke. He was humble. Wouldn't that be a change for the better? She thought of her dad—always extolling his superiority in the boardroom, on the golf course or at the dinner table. Her brother was a chip off the old block. And Kip? She winced at the memory of her rocky year dating a man who turned out to be exactly like her father.

"Oh, there's the music lady," one of the twins called out. Standing side by side, they were identical from their sleek blond hair, heart-shaped faces all the way to their black heels. They wore different dresses—one blue and the other lilac—but the style was the same.

"I'll go help!" The twin in lilac broke away, tapping down the aisle toward a woman hefting a cello case.

"Well, kids." Lil clapped her hands. "Time to get this show on the road. Hunter, you have your checklist?"

"I'll get busy." The darker, burlier version of Luke gave a grim nod, pulled a piece of paper from his pocket and left.

"Luke? You'll make sure the musicians are set up?" Lil gave her chair a turn. "The rest of you, come with me."

"Jerrod, why don't you...?"

"Sit here and finish reading *A Farewell to Arms?*" he finished, crooking one eyebrow.

She laughed. "You are a funny kid. I was going to say why don't you go sit outside?"

"Really?"

"As long as you stay close, I don't see why not. Keep within sight of the front door."

"Cool." He reached in his pocket and hauled out his iPod.

"I can keep an eye on him." Luke's voice rumbled near her ear. "I'll be seating guests."

"I'd appreciate that. I was hoping there would be kids his age here."

"Bree's fiancé, Mac, has a teenage brother. Probably a few years older, but Marcus is a good kid. They might get along just fine."

"Good. I like your family, Luke."

"They're all right. I'll keep 'em." A faint blush crept across his high cheekbones. "Although I am sorry. They took a lot of interest in you. I'm afraid they think—"

"—that you and I are an item?"

"Yep. And when they get you alone, they might, uh—"

"—try to sell me on you for my boyfriend?"

He nodded, relieved that she understood.

"Don't worry. I'm from a big family, too. I totally get it." She tried to ignore the pinch of pain she felt every time she thought of her family.

"You haven't written about your family much." His tone dipped pleasantly. "At least you haven't shared them with me."

"Guilty." Another painful pinch. "Let's just say my parents aren't happy with me. I feel the same toward them."

"Ah, I've been there." The pinch of sadness creasing his face spoke the truth, but she couldn't picture it.

"I don't believe it. Your family is great."

"I'm talking about my folks. Mom—" He hesitated, as if needing strength to talk about it. "Let's just say we don't know if she's going to show up today for Brooke's wedding. She wanted Brooke to come to Miles City to get married. And then there's Dad—"

He fell silent and shook his head. A muscle jumped

along his jaw. "Dad got out of federal prison not too long ago. He's made bad choices in his life, and one of them is how he treats people. We're praying he doesn't show up today."

"Nothing can hurt like family." She reached out to squeeze his hand, meaning to let him know he wasn't alone, she knew exactly how that felt, but a snap of awareness jolted through her at the first brush of her skin to his. His strong fingers curled around hers, holding on, and the snap deepened. It became an emotional hook that dug into her heart.

Really weird, she thought. *What was happening?* Before she could analyze it, Luke released her hand, unhooked her heart and the snap of awareness faded.

"You say that like you know." Luke hiked up his shoulders like a man determined to handle a tough situation. "I thought you were good with your family."

"No family is perfect, although mine tries to be." She glanced down the aisle to where sunshine gleamed on the wood floor. On the other side of the open double doors, Jerrod sat hunched over his player, sitting on the front step as promised. Did she really want to talk about her past? "I don't miss that, but I miss them."

"I always wondered if there was more to your story than you were telling me. You didn't come to Montana to work just because Mrs. Lambert is your mother's friend, right? There's another reason."

Too personal, she wanted to tell him. She'd been careful during their correspondence to keep things safe. That's how she wanted life these days—safe, predictable and level. But one look at the caring on his perfectly chiseled face, and she knew why he had been so easy to chat with online and why she looked forward to his emails. Luke McKaslin was a caring man. She'd been with him in person for less than ten minutes and it shone through as clear as daylight.

She felt comfortable enough with him to admit the truth. "We had a disagreement over whether or not I should give my boyfriend back his engagement ring."

"Your b-boyfriend?" He stumbled over the word. "Now that's something I didn't know."

"I didn't mean to keep it from you. I simply didn't want to talk about it." She gave a little shrug. "Too painful. Besides, he's my ex-boyfriend now, which is the reason my family is disappointed in me."

"And that's why you left California?"

"Mrs. Lambert was looking for a tutor, she was moving to their summer home and I thought, perfect timing. Why not?" She'd been substituting and the offer had been the chance for a steady paycheck. "God seemed to be nudging me along, so I packed up and came."

"I'm glad you did, otherwise we never would have met."

"Ditto." She liked his smile, she decided. It was his most impressive feature, and there were many of those to choose from. "I can't say that I'm glad I'm stuck in Montana, but something good has come out of this."

"Maybe after you have fun with us and get in your social time, you'll change your mind about Montana?" He arched one eyebrow in a challenge.

"It's going to take more than that. I'm not sure it can be done," she quipped, taking a step backward, moving away from him. "But I'm liking the chance to actually make new friends."

"Good. I'm going to change your mind."

"Is that a warning or a threat?"

"Depends on which one will work."

"Neither." She tipped back her head and laughed.

"I'm not going to change my mind. I'm a California girl. I miss the beach. There's no beach in Montana. No ocean."

"True, but we've got riverbanks."

"So not the same."

They laughed together. He liked Honor as much in real life as he had online. His throat tightened, making it hard to swallow as he watched her walk away. A swirl of her blue dress's hem, a clip of her fancy shoes and a flip of her sleek honey hair and he was hooked just a little bit more.

It's never going to happen, he told himself. Did that stop him from liking her more?

Not a chance.

"Honor, there you are!" Brooke popped her head out of the inner door. "Don't think I'm going to let you out of your offer."

"Good, because I was beginning to worry you were starting without me."

"Not a chance." Brooke shone with happiness. She'd had some tough times, but God had turned those hardships around. He'd brought Liam into her life, and for that Luke would always be grateful. Brooke deserved true love and a happily-ever-after.

"Luke? What are you doing standing there?" Brooke flashed her smile his way. "Guests are arriving!"

"Wow, I guess so." He glanced over his shoulder at the familiar faces of his cousins coming up the steps. A photographer waved at him from the back, setting up. He had things to do, but he stole one moment longer to take in the sight of Honor Crosby as she hurried up to Brooke. The two women talked low, their voices a ring of merriment. Honor's gentle alto stood out above the other sounds in the church. His heart gave a little lurch.

She slipped through the doorway and out of his sight. He raked a hand through his hair, wishing he didn't feel anything at all for her. Just wishing he was in control of his emotions.

"Hey, Luke." Cousin Spence McKaslin ambled up and clapped him on the shoulder. "We're glad this day has come for Brooke. No one deserves happiness more."

"That's the general consensus. Glad you could make it. Hi, Lucy," he greeted Spence's blond-haired, sunny wife. "It's good to see you again."

"We wouldn't miss this wedding for the world. I didn't see a table set up for gifts anywhere." She held up a beautifully wrapped box. "Where can I put this?"

"That was on my to-do list. Sorry." He dug in his pocket for the paper Lil had written out for him. Best get to it. "I'll take that for you."

"I'll seat them." Mac, Bree's fiancé, ambled up in his suit and tie. "Spence, I was just in your bookstore the other day…"

As the trio headed up the aisle, Luke's thoughts turned to Honor. How was she faring being stuck in a room with his sisters? And what exactly were they talking about?

He thought of Lil, dear Lil, and hoped his name didn't come up because he knew what the subject would be.

Chapter Three

"**P**oor Luke. He has been single for so long." Lil held out the gossamer bridal veil. "Ever since Sonya."

"Sonya." Brooke shook her head, obviously disapproving of this former girlfriend. "She led him on and then let him down."

"That's too bad," Honor said sympathetically, trying not to sound too interested. It would only prolong the discussion, the one that would extol all of Luke's virtues as a possible future boyfriend.

A boyfriend she didn't want. No way, no sir. She was a happily single woman these days and that's the way it was going to stay. She grabbed the comb off the built-in dresser.

"He's the sweetest guy." Brooke ducked, awaiting her veil.

"The sweetest," Cousin Katherine agreed as she took the veil carefully from Lil.

Brooke nodded. "I never thought he would get over what that woman did to him."

"Neither did I," Colbie agreed.

"Us, too," the twins chimed in.

What did that woman do? Honor wanted to ask, but

she was afraid to. The women surrounding her might see it as a sign of interest. *Romantic* interest. She doubted they understood the friend thing she and Luke had going on. Maybe a change of subject was in order.

"Aren't you nervous, Brooke?" she said the first thing that popped into her head. "Do you have cold feet? A jittery stomach?"

"No, not a bit. Everything is calm and my feet are warm." Brooke stopped to check her reflection in the mirror. "I've never been so sure of anything in my life, and stop trying to change the subject."

"Hey, a girl's gotta try." She held up her hands in a what-can-I-do gesture. "You look stunning."

"It's the dress. Colbie and Lil made it for me." Brooke brushed at the delicate satin of the princess-cut gown, which showed off her willowy figure adorably. "I never thought I would be the one to marry before you, Bree."

"You know I want a spring wedding," the twin in blue answered dreamily. "Now that I'm engaged and Brooke is getting married, I wonder who will be next?"

"Not me," Colbie announced as she stepped back to check the drape of the wedding dress and gave a single, satisfied nod. "It's the single life for me."

"Me, too!" Finally, a comrade in arms! A like-minded ally.

"Oh, you two." Lil shook her head. "I'm disappointed in you. Love can be the greatest adventure. You have to keep your heart open for it."

"I'll keep mine closed, thank you very much." Colbie's violet eyes sparkled with humor. "I prefer to be closed-up. It keeps the troublemakers away."

"And men tend to be troublemakers," Honor agreed.

"I can't argue there." Katherine finished pinning the veil and stepped back to admire her work. "When I first met Jack, disaster. Trouble of the highest magnitude. His teenage daughter had shoplifted from the bookstore and I had to march out into the parking lot and tell him so while he was in his uniform sitting in his cruiser."

"I mistook Brice for a burglar," a voice added cheerfully as a door swung open. A blond beauty stood in the doorway. "Hysterical. I've never lived it down. I've been sent in to tell you everything is ready out there. The guests are seated. The minister is ready to go. The quartet is playing."

"Wonderful. We'll bring the bride right out, Ava dear."

"Okay! Don't worry, Brooke. No need to be nervous." Ava propped the door open before she left. "Getting married is the most amazing feeling. I'm so happy for you."

"She's our boss at the bakery," the twin in the lavender explained.

"She's also our cousin," the blue twin added. "Are you ready, Brooke?"

"Absolutely." Brooke looked ethereal with bliss as she took one final look in the mirror. "I'm breathless."

"You're a princess, my dear," Lil enthused. "Just perfect."

"Flawless."

"Beautiful."

The McKaslin sisters chimed their compliments, gathered around the bride, clearly about to line up for the procession. Time to find Jerrod in the church and settle in for the ceremony. Honor slipped out the door, unable to look away as the sisters embraced the bride, their happy voices echoing down the hallway.

That never would have been me, she thought as she tripped into the vestibule. She never would have felt joyful marrying Kip. Just the proof she'd needed to know she made the right decision.

"Honor." Luke offered her his arm, the consummate groomsman. "May I escort you to your seat?"

"I would love that." As she slipped her arm through his, emotion fluttered in her heart. Light, sweet and full of peace, that feeling stayed with her as she stumbled forward at his side, her feet barely touching the ground.

This is what I get for skipping breakfast, she thought as she seemed to float down the aisle. Light-headed, shivery, quick, swooping pulse. Those were definitely signs of low blood sugar and not romantic interest, and they were easily remedied. Big relief there.

"Don't believe a single word they said about me," he advised.

"You mean you're not nice? You're not a good guy?"

"Okay, I sure try to be." A grin carved into his features, softening the rugged planes of his face and bringing out those swoon-worthy dimples. "But I'm sure that wasn't the gist of the conversation."

"How did you know you were even mentioned?"

"Uh, cuz my sisters meddle. Lil is the worst."

"They did happen to mention you were single and available, but don't worry, I thwarted them at every turn by changing the subject."

"Did it work?"

"Eventually. I'm persistent. Others see it as stubborn, but that's not entirely a bad thing." A little breathless, she was glad when Luke stopped at the end of a row. "I finally steered the conversation back to the bride. She looks beautiful, by the way, so prepare yourself."

"I have no doubt."

Luke's eyes had little flecks of gold in them, stunning against the violet-blue, so stunning she couldn't seem to look away. Definitely strange, too, she thought, more light-headed, still. Perhaps she'd break into the candy she kept in the bottom of her purse. That ought to chase away her symptoms. She slipped her arm from his. "Thank you for escorting me."

"My pleasure."

Oh, but those dimples could dazzle any woman. Good thing they didn't have an effect on her. No way, no how. Her shoes tapped against the floor as she scooted into the row. "I'll see you after?"

"I'll hang back so you can follow me," Luke said as he pivoted, talking over his shoulder. "I drive a white truck. Don't worry, I'll keep an eye out for you in the parking lot."

"Thanks," she said, but he was gone, hurrying to seat a latecoming guest.

The other groomsmen were lined up at the front, the groom a calm, content-looking man who joked with his best man. The low rumble of their laughter blended with the din of the crowd and the rise and fall of notes from the quartet. Finally the crowd hushed as the minister took his place and the processional music began.

"Are you sure the cake will be good?" Jerrod whispered to her as he put his iPod on pause. Apparently he knew where his priorities were.

"Positively."

As quietly as she could, she unlatched her handbag and dug out a roll of candy. She offered it to Jerrod first, who happily took a few, ripped the paper farther down on the roll and popped the sweet-tart lozenge into her mouth. Flavor exploded on her tongue. Take that, low blood sugar.

An adorable little girl with bouncy brown curls paraded down the aisle, tossing rose petals from her fancy white basket. She looked like a cherub with angelic cheeks and sweet button face. Her snowy lacy dress swung around her knees. Completely adorable.

"That's Madison, my niece," whispered the woman who'd visited the dressing room. The baker, cousin Ava, leaned over the back of the pew, eyes wide with curiosity. "Isn't she adorable? I hear you are dating Luke?"

"Not dating," she corrected way too fast and way too defensive. Best to blame that on the low blood sugar, too. "Everyone has the wrong idea. Luke and I are just friends."

"Sure. I know what you mean. That's the best place to start."

Not sure how to argue with that, she held her tongue. The little ring bearer strode down the aisle, a cute little boy sure of his duty.

"My nephew, Tyler," Ava informed her.

The bridesmaids came next, strolling down the aisle carrying bouquets of daisies. Each dress was a different color—blue, lilac and gold. When they reached the front, Honor noticed Luke standing alongside the best man, shoulders set, back straight, striking in his dark suit. Incredibly fine-looking.

Her heart gave another swoop, so she popped a second candy into her mouth. That was absolutely the last time she was skipping breakfast.

Exultation flitted in the air like the scent of roses from a nearby border row as friends and family descended the church stairs and streamed toward their vehicles, buckled in and zoomed off. Honor beeped the remote, her car door locks popped and Jerrod dropped into the passenger seat. She went up on tiptoe, looking around for a sign of Luke. White pickup, he'd said. She frowned, seeing at least ten white trucks gleaming in the lot. Now what?

"Over here!" called a familiar voice.

She whirled around, shading her eyes with her hand as she squinted into the hot noon sun. "There you are. Did you know there are at least a dozen white pickups in this lot?"

"Sorry." He eased behind the wheel, leaving the door open so he could holler across the roof of a departing car. "I'd planned on finding you in the crowd, but you made a fast dash toward the exit."

"It was hard not to. It was like being a salmon in a river current. I decided to go with the flow."

"The McKaslins and friends are a desperate bunch when we get hungry."

"I know, right?" She slipped into the leather seat, scorching from sitting in the sun. Yikes. Her fingers seared when she touched the steering wheel. "Is it very far?"

If so, she'd likely melt.

"Not too far. Follow me."

She eyed the mad dash of vehicles toward the exit. "I'll try."

"Not to worry. I'll keep my eye on you." He winked. Why did the man have to have a dazzling wink, too? His door closed and his truck's engine roared to life.

"I'm dying," Jerrod commented. "Air conditioning. Quick."

"I doubt it will help in time. We may be a puddle of carbon-based goo before we reach the street."

"No kidding." Jerrod fanned himself, not that it would help, and whizzed down his window. The instant the engine turned over, he took charge of the a/c controls.

"So, not too bad so far, right?" She buckled up.

"At least we're out of the house." Jerrod frowned at the hot air spewing from the vents. "You're sure there'll be kids my age here?"

"That's the word." She checked her mirror, saw the grill of Luke's truck lumbering closer and smiled in spite of herself. "You miss your friends back home."

"You know it." Jerrod leaned forward to catch the tepid air from the vents.

Luke motored by in his gleaming truck. She caught a flash of his smile as she pulled out to get in behind him. Here's where her California driving skills came in handy. She nosed in front of a Buick jockeying for supremacy and angled in behind Luke's tailgate. Skills honed from mall parking lots. Good to know they hadn't gone rusty.

Her cell chimed. She scrambled for the Bluetooth earpiece and answered before it went to voice mail. "Hello?"

"Nice maneuvering back there. That was the minister's car."

"Oops!" She felt a twinge of guilt as she glanced in her rearview at the Buick idling behind her. "Between that and missing all but one percent of Sunday service, I'm in need of serious penance."

"I'll say. And before you ask, there's not an afternoon service you can catch."

"How did you know I was going to ask?" She flipped on her right blinker when his started to blink.

"I know you don't like to miss church."

"That's right." How many Sunday mornings had she ended a chat session because she needed to dash off to church? "It's weird because you and I know each other, but at the same time we don't. We're strangers who are, well, strangers."

"True. We just technically met." His trunk made a neat turn onto the street.

She pulled up, took advantage of the clear road and turned after him. "So, tell me about where we're going. You mentioned volleyball."

"Shh. That's top secret, remember? If anyone asks—"

"—I'll deny any knowledge—"

"—or you'll be disavowed."

"Why do I suddenly want to hum the *Mission: Impossible* theme?"

"I don't know, but I have the same urge."

This was why she'd liked typing at Luke. He was fun. She scooted through a yellow light keeping on his tail, breezing through the intersection before the red. Perfect timing. "So, how does the volleyball team selection work in your family?"

"Don't worry. When we choose sides, I'll call you first."

"You're just going on my word that I can play. What if I'm exaggerating or have an overinflated opinion of my own skills?"

"That's a risk I'm ready to take."

"Aren't those fateful words? Like pride goeth before a fall? Doom happens when you least expect it?"

"And here I thought you were an optimist. A glass-half-full kind of girl."

"It depends on the day," she quipped, following him through a housing development. "I'm always more positive on a full stomach. We were running late, so I missed breakfast."

"The truth comes out. The concrete irrigation pipe being transported wasn't the only reason you were late."

"I was hoping you wouldn't bring it up, but yes. I couldn't decide what to wear. It's been so long since I really got to dress up." She scooted into a spot at the curb behind his truck. A slope of lush lawn led the way to a lovely brick Tudor, shaded by maples. Must be their destination. She hated turning off the engine, now that the a/c was finally blowing glacial cold.

"You're one of those fashionista types, aren't you? Always shopping?"

"Could be, but I've known worse." She gave Jerrod a nod, who opened his door and spilled out into the heat. "I'm nothing like my mom and sisters. They are serious fashion divas."

"And you are—"

"—a mild clothes fanatic. Nothing compared to if you put me in a bookstore, then look out." She opened the door to sunshine.

"Same here." Luke, towering over her, flipped his phone shut and held out his hand. "I can't walk outta there without doing some damage."

"Don't expect me to find anything wrong with that." She placed her hand in his, palm to palm and—zap! There went that zing of emotion charging through her again.

See, it has to be low blood sugar—again, she thought as she rose from her seat. The candy was out of her system, which was crashing. Proof she needed lunch and needed it fast. Because it definitely, absolutely, under no circumstances could be related to the fact that handsome, impressive, drop-dead gorgeous Luke McKaslin was holding her hand.

Probably best to ignore the fact that the sensation stopped when she released his hand.

"This is the groom's grandfather's home." Luke led the way up a few steps. A curving walkway ribboned through grass to the shady sanctuary of the charming house. "He was generous enough to host the reception. I don't think he truly understood what he was getting into, the poor man."

"Yes, since I've met some of your family. Shockingly scary."

"Tell me about it." Luke rolled his eyes. On the front porch, a swing squeaked. A couple sat hand in hand watching over the little kids playing soccer on the large side yard. "Hey, Danielle. Jonas."

"Hey, yourself," the handsome, dark-haired man answered. "Didn't know you were bringing a date."

"I'm not," Luke answered easily, opening the screen door for her. "This is my friend, Honor."

"Hi, Honor," Danielle smiled warmly. "A friend, huh?"

"Inside quick," Luke whispered in her ear, steering her and they tumbled inside the gracious foyer, chuckling together. "I thought they would be better behaved about this, but I'm afraid this is only the beginning. It's sort of embarrassing."

"Don't worry about it. They mean well." She remembered the caring way his sisters and Lil had talked about him in the dressing room. Clearly his family loved him.

"That's the problem. You know what they say about good intentions? That's one road that can lead to no place good." He took her by the elbow and steered her past a crowded living room, which opened to the right. Several "Hi, Luke"s rang out and a bold, "Aren't you going to introduce us to your girl?" They kept going, bypassing the kitchen, too. Caterers bustled around marble counters and sunshine sparkled on a wall of windows, leading the way to the deck.

"Maybe you want to escape while you can or disavow all knowledge of me." Luke released her elbow.

"It's tempting." She took a step back, surveying the man and the French door he held open for her. Maybe the zinging sensation she kept feeling had nothing to do with low blood sugar.

Wasn't that a frightening thought?

The sun kissed her with its blazing warmth as she tapped her way across the spacious deck. Across the stretch of lawn, a pool glistened to the right. A volleyball net staked out a section of grass to the left and the laughing shrieks of children rang in the distance as little kids ran around clutching helium balloons. One slipped away and wafted up in the air. The beauty who'd been the flower girl tipped her head back, curls swinging, to watch it fly away. A yellow Labrador bounded up to her and kissed her cheek.

The delicious scent of barbecue smoke drifted on the breeze from a built-in grill. An elderly man stood behind it, a long handled spatula in hand. Must be the groom's grandfather.

"Come and get it," he called heartily. "Lunch is ready."

"Just in time. My stomach is grumbling." As proof, it gurgled. "Embarrassing."

"Or perfect timing." Luke leaned in, the smoky notes in his voice ringing low and mesmerizing. "C'mon. In this family you snooze, you lose. The McKaslins love their food."

"So I see." Caterers buzzed in and out of the kitchen,

migrating to two cloth-covered tables loaded with choices.

She took the plate Luke handed her and scooped a hot dog bun out of the bag. Little kids ran by her, looking for their moms. The yellow dog bounded after them, skidded to a stop, lifted his nose into the air and breathed deep.

"Don't even think about it, Oscar." Liam, the groom, grabbed the Lab by his collar. "Good behavior, remember? Or you'll be banned to the house."

Oscar's head tilted, he gave a whine of apology and irresistible chocolate eyes blinked sadly.

"C'mon, I'll get an extra hot dog for you." Liam seemed like a really nice guy, kind and strong. A very nice combination. She thought of gentle, sweet Brooke and nodded. It was a good match. A very good one, indeed. The newlyweds met in the center of the deck. Soft touches, loving smiles and rippling laughter.

Just the way love should be. Again, she thought of Kip and the wedding he'd wanted—big, fancy, expensive, a showcase. Without love, it would have been a shell of what a real wedding ought to be. She'd definitely done the right thing in fleeing Malibu even if she wasn't exactly happy here.

She caught sight of Jerrod ambling into view with a taller, older teen boy carrying a soccer ball. Jerrod looked as though he was having a good time. *Good,* she thought. *Exactly what he needed.*

"What would you like, missy?" the elderly gentleman asked, his spatula poised and ready over the grill.

She eyed her choices.

"A hot dog, please," she said with a smile, laughing when Luke held out his plate for one, too.

They were so alike, it was kind of fun. She was so,

so glad she'd decided to come. Here, with Luke, she didn't miss home. He was exactly the friend in person he'd been online. She couldn't ask for more than that.

Chapter Four

Laughter dominated the conversation buzzing around her as she took a bite of her hotdog. She couldn't help taking a moment to drink it all in. Happiness buzzed in the air, family and friends chatted, laughed, joked. Best of all, the happy newlyweds sat together, their happiness so infectious it made Honor start to think love wasn't such a bad thing, after all.

"This isn't the kind of wedding reception you're used to, is it?" Luke dragged a potato chip through a puddle of dip on his plate.

"You have no idea." She reached for her cup of punch, sucked it down and reached for the mustard bottle. "You have no idea what I'm used to."

"Enlighten me."

"Not sure you're tough enough to handle it." She eyed the man beside her at the picnic table, considered his muscled form and shook her head. "No, I don't think you can. Most men run."

"I'm not most men. Give it a shot. Just see if I bolt."

"You do look tougher than most." She didn't have to ask to know Luke's strength wasn't honed in a gym but through hard, physical work. "I knew something was off the instant I walked into church."

"Off?" A dimple etched into his cheek.

She really needed to stop noticing his dimples. "Where were the nerves, the tempers and the frantic craziness? When my oldest sister got married, we lived in a frenetic state for four months pre-wedding."

"Was it a fancy wedding?"

"An exquisite one." She squirted mustard along the length of the bun in an even stripe. "A fairy tale come true. The wedding planner had to hire extra help to pull it all."

"Sounds like a fancy affair."

"The fanciest." She didn't mention her father was one of the most sought after financial managers in the state. His clientele ranged from movie stars to corporate multimillionaires.

"Something tells me you were expecting something spiffier." The wind ruffled Luke's thick, sandy hair. "Hope we didn't disappoint. I did warn you."

"I've been to a lot of spiffy weddings." All three of her sisters' weddings, cousins, friends, her father's clients. "Not one has been as genuine as this one. Brooke and Liam clearly love one another."

"They do."

Silence fell between them. At the next picnic table over, the bride and groom nestled together, sharing a private moment despite the family surrounding them. The groom leaned in to whisper something, and Brooke's smile blossomed and the love that filled her eyes when she gazed upon her new husband was singular. Never had Honor seen anything as pure and true.

"And here I've vowed to stop believing in the existence of true love." She dug her fork into the remnants of potato salad on her plate.

"I know what you mean," Luke agreed.

"Those two had to prove me wrong." She sighed a little, watching the couple. "What am I going to do now? Start believing again?"

"Brooke and Liam have that effect," he agreed lightly. "Where did your disillusionment come from, your former fiancé?"

"Partly. Marriage is a big business in my family. Not that there isn't love." She looked quick to clarify. "But money trumps love if it ever comes down to it. You should have seen my parents' divorce."

"Mine was pretty ugly, too." He blocked out those old memories. Not worth thinking about. It was why he'd always thought long and hard before getting serious in a relationship. Not that it was a fail-safe plan. Sonya had broken his heart. Love could turn out better, like it had for Brooke and for his other sister, Bree, but there was a pattern in his family. One of romantic disaster. He was afraid of repeating it.

Picking the right woman seemed to be the key, he'd decided. The trick was in finding her.

"That's why I'm single." She took a small bite of hot dog. "I worried that Kip and I didn't have what it took to make it last. There were too many problems."

"Like what?"

"Just about everything." She swiped a dab of mustard from her lip.

Pretty lip. He leaned in a little closer, wanting to hear her better. The rest of the party faded away, the din of cheerful conversations silenced until there was only Honor with the breeze tousling her hair and the golden sunshine adoring her. Zip, there she was. The center of his attention.

"Kip went to college with my sister and one day she bumped into him, found out he was all alone on the West Coast without family and invited him to Thanksgiving dinner." She set down her hot dog and picked up her fork. "He was charming and his interest in me was flattering. When he called me up a week later to ask me out, I accepted."

"Was he a nice guy?"

"He was. He was also really ambitious." She shrugged her shoulders in a what-can-you-do gesture. "He was polite, he worked hard to ingratiate himself with my family and he seemed happy to be with me. It seemed like the sort of relationship I'd been hoping for."

"You're using 'seemed' a lot. I get the sense that was the problem."

"Exactly. He did everything right and he said everything right, but something felt off. Something felt missing. I didn't know what. I just chalked it up to him being so busy with his work. My father liked him and had offered him a job. Which was his goal all along, apparently."

"Oh, I get it. He'd set his sights on the boss's daughter."

"And not really me." A dash of pain flashed in her eyes, but she shrugged it away. She'd been hurt.

He hated that. He knew what it was like to find out the one you were falling in love with wasn't as devoted as you thought. "How did you find out?"

"It was the first time we met with our wedding planner. He kept texting, answering his phone, leaving to sort out some problem at work. He had a high-pressure job, I got it, but when he came back and was sitting near me, he wasn't there. He was bored, not with the plans but with me. It wasn't me he loved."

"It was the successful life he was trying to build?"

"That's it." Her hand landed on his arm, reaching out to him.

As he looked down at her slender fingers against the white cuff of his shirtsleeve, his heart tripped.

"Kip never actually loved me. It wasn't that he didn't care, it was more that I was a necessary step to what he wanted his life to be," she explained. "As my husband, his future at the company would be secure."

"Ouch." He winced, understanding. She'd loved the man and wanted his love in return. He'd been in a similar situation.

"After the wedding planner, we had a heart-to-heart. Kip didn't have time to talk, so we argued and in his anger the truth spilled out. I was stunned."

"Did you break off the engagement right away?"

"Yes, but my family pressured me to reconsider. Everyone loved him. He fit in so well. My sisters and mom kept saying it was just wedding jitters, that what I was feeling was perfectly normal. After the wedding I would be a happy bride. Not to worry."

"I'm glad you didn't give in."

"Me, too. I didn't want to marry a man who loved success more than he would love me. My family was devastated with my decision."

"They love you. They must want what's best for you."

"They were convinced Kip was it. That's the hard part." She stirred her fork around in the remains of her potato salad, and he could feel how hard it had been for her.

"It must have taken a lot of courage to stand up for what you wanted with all that well-meaning pressure."

"I don't know about courage, but it wasn't easy. That's why I took the job tutoring Jerrod. It got me away from the situation. I could regroup, figure out what I wanted and get my head together."

And the pieces of her heart, he figured. He knew how that felt, too. "Is it working?"

"I'll let you know." She smiled, nothing could be prettier. His pulse fluttered, because he'd never seen a more beautiful woman. Her expressive blue eyes just blew him away.

"Hey, you two!" Colbie trotted over, changed into a T-shirt, athletic shorts and tennis shoes. "Let the game begin. Girls against guys."

"No way." He dropped his fork on his plate. "We talked about this, remember? Honor's on my team."

"Not anymore. As the entertainment director of this reception, I have unilaterally changed my mind. Sorry, buddy." Colbie winked at him. "This is for Honor's own good."

"My own good?" Honor sounded surprised as she took a last sip of punch. "Is Luke a terrible player?"

"No, but we're better. This way you'll be on the winning team, and we'll get to know you better." Colbie gave a wink and bounded off to drum up more players for the match.

"This is already spiraling out of control." Luke shook his head. "That's what happens when a woman takes over."

"I'm sure if your sister heard that and believed you meant it, she wouldn't take that well." Honor hopped up from the bench, reached over to steal his plate and stacked hers on top. "I'll take these in. I need to change. I don't want to play in my dress."

Before he could answer, she breezed away. Brandi

caught up to her, asking her about who designed her dress, some fancy name he'd never heard before, and the pair tapped off in the direction of the house, leaving him behind like he was yesterday's laundry.

Well, at least he knew where he stood. He shook his head, pushed off the bench and dodged his cousin's son, dashing off to play with the other little kids in the sprinkler. Around him rang the happiness of his family, who were still seated and relaxed, talking merrily.

"She's nice." Colbie returned to sidle up to him. "Are you mad about the team thing?"

"Not mad, but something tells me you guessed she was a ringer."

"Bingo. I see that look in your eye. You care for her." Colbie patted him on the arm.

"And here I hoped it didn't show."

"You have two choices. You can try harder to hide it or you could let her know."

"She doesn't feel the same way I do."

"Yet." Love gentled her words. Colbie was a great sister, always looking out for him. "Maybe she'll change her mind."

"No, and it's just as well. She's leaving for home in a few weeks." He caught a glimpse of her through the open French doors, where she stood in the kitchen stacking the plates on the counter and chatting with Uncle John.

Honor was a city girl and not the farm girl he was looking for. Not the kind of woman who would fit into his life on the ranch. His chest ached with disappointment, but he'd known that about her all along.

It was his heart giving him troubles, because his head knew for absolute certain she was not the woman for him.

"You'd better go change." Colbie's sympathy gentled her words. "And don't be sad. The right woman is out there. I know it. You deserve the very best."

"So do you." He gave her hand a squeeze.

"I don't believe it! You don't like Montana?" Bree spiked the ball, sending it flying over the net. The other team members jockeyed into position as the blur that was the ball soared straight up in the air.

"It's not that I don't like Montana, it's that I don't get Montana," Honor explained as she punched the ball and it arced over the net.

"What's not to get?" Kelly, Luke's cousin, asked as her husband, Mitch, volleyed the ball back to Honor's side.

"Where's the beach?" She rocked up on her heels, watching as Colbie dove for the save. "Where's the ocean? Where's the mall?"

"No ocean or beach, but we've got a mall," Colbie quipped as she sent the ball up into the air.

"Two hours' drive away from the Lamberts'. Four round trip." She moved in to smack the ball with her fist, sending it flying straight at Luke. He was simply where her gaze went. Where she naturally aimed the ball. This wasn't the first time.

He knocked it back, his violet-blue gaze so intense it was all she could see. She tripped over her own feet and wham! Down she went. When she hit the ground shock ricocheted along her bones as her knee rammed into the earth. The ball thudded next to her.

"Are you okay?" Colbie towered over her, grabbed the ball. "You went down so fast, I couldn't do anything."

"It won't be the first time I've tripped over my feet."

She sat up and a shadow tumbled over her. A tall, broad-shouldered shadow. Her breathing hitched when she squinted up at Luke, who offered his hand.

"Let's get you up and see the damage." His fingers wrapped around hers. "You weren't kidding about being a klutz. I didn't believe you."

"I can be a hazard to myself." She found herself rising through the air and on her feet, breathless from the ascent. Maybe, just maybe, she had to admit, it may have something to do with the man. His callused palm, his touch, the snap of feeling that went way too deep.

"You're bleeding." Luke released her.

The zing faded predictably. When he knelt down to inspect her knee she had to face facts. She could no longer blame her reaction to him on low blood sugar. Didn't that spell trouble?

"Doesn't look too bad. Mostly just grass burn. You've scraped a few layers off." Luke gazed up at her, his head tilted back, exposing the whirl of a cowlick at his crown. "What we need is a Band-Aid."

"I'm tough. I don't need a bandage." Her voice sounded thick to her own ears and a little breathless. A bandage might up the chance of Luke touching her again. What she didn't want was to prove her hypothesis. That this man affected her in ways she wasn't ready for. It would be best to deny it, if she could. "What I need is to score the winning point. We're almost there."

"Yeah!" agreed Colbie, one arm around the ball, balanced on her hip. "As long as Honor's okay, let's do it. You men are toast."

"Hold up one minute." Not to be rushed, Luke held up one hand. Only then did Honor notice his Aunt Dorrie hurrying over with a box clutched in one hand.

"I saw you go down, dear." She bustled up, panting

a little. "This was all I could find on short notice. Do you need an antibacterial cream?"

"Thank you." It was hard not to like Luke's family. "It's just a scratch, so I should be fine."

"Good. I wouldn't want this to put a kink in your date. There's nothing like a wedding date." Dorrie's eyes sparkled, she handed Luke the box and patted Honor's cheek. Kind, thoughtful, completely lovable. "So glad you're here."

Definitely impossible not to like.

"This won't hurt a bit." With a crackle, Luke freed a Band-Aid from its wrapper and knelt before her. She knew both teams watched, that everything had come to a standstill the moment Luke had rushed to her side of the net. That didn't stop her heart from wobbling dangerously as the big, tough Montana cowboy applied the bandage to her knee with care. At the warm brush of his fingertips against her kneecap, the zing returned so strong, dizziness rushed through her head.

There's only one solution, she thought. *Stop with the touching.*

"There." Luke rose up to his six-foot-plus height, shading her from the sun. Light danced around him, burnishing gold highlights into his sandy hair. Irresistible.

Whoops, where had that thought come from? It was a big mistake. She needed a friend. But the way he was looking at her with more than concern and a lot of caring totally panicked her. What were his expectations? What was he hoping for?

Worse, what if he'd been hoping for more than friendship with her?

"Guess I'll get back to my side," he said, backing

away, taking his shadow with him. The sun tumbled over her, too bright suddenly for her eyes.

I wish I was ready to believe again, she thought as Colby's hand settled on her shoulder. *To put faith in love.*

"Sure you're okay?" she asked, as if she was wondering about more than the skinned knee.

"I'm great." She cleared her throat and wished she didn't feel a twinge of emotion. "Let's finish this."

"As victors," Colbie agreed with an understanding smile. She seemed to notice everything that had gone on and didn't judge. Just cared.

Yes, she absolutely wished she was ready for a relationship that was more than friendship. Judging by the panic racing through her veins, she wasn't even close.

"Let's go!" Luke's cousin Aubrey called as she caught the ball, stepping back to serve.

"C'mon, we can do this!" Lucy cheered. "Three more points."

"Two after this," Aubrey said as she served, sending the ball streaking over the net. The opposing team dove, but failed to set it. It whammed against the ground, cheers went up, but all Honor could see was Luke. His rugged stance and the remembered caring she'd seen.

What was she going to do about that?

With the women's shouts and woo-hoos of delight at their victory peppering the air, Luke dove around the net posts, heading straight for his target. "How's the knee?"

"Nothing to worry about. I'm more concerned about your ego." Honor tossed her ponytail over one shoulder—she'd tied back her hair for the match. "Losing to a bunch of girls. That can be tough for a guy."

"This guy's used to it." He let his eyes twinkle at her. He wanted her to know he wasn't one of those insecure men. "You have some skills. Your church league must miss you."

"I miss them." She waltzed alongside him, her sneakers rasping in the soft lawn. "But it won't be much longer. I'm counting the days."

"I wish we'd met on the front end of your sentence in Montana."

"Sentence? At times that has felt exactly right, but other times, like today, well, let's just say Montana has had its moments."

"Glad to hear it. I wouldn't want you leaving with a dim view of us." The afternoon was flying by and if she wanted to get Jerrod home by supper, then she had to get on the road. He ignored the hitch in his chest. "You look like you had a good time."

"Absolutely." She sparkled, as bright as the sun. "Thanks for inviting me. I needed it."

"Got some social time in?"

"Did I. And invitations for more." She glanced over her shoulder where his sisters and cousins were tromping toward the punch bowl, their laughter as carefree as the breeze. "You have a fun family."

"Thanks, I think so, too."

"And I'm so grateful for your friendship." Sincerity deepened the hue of her eyes. Genuine caring shone there, but it wasn't what he hoped for.

It was, however, what he'd expected. Friends. Yes, he got the message. Her kind, caring, gentle message as her hand caught his. Recognition flared in his heart, as if he'd been waiting for her his whole life. But he tamped it down, knowing a lost cause when he saw it.

"I'm grateful for yours," he choked out, sounding

almost completely normal so she would never know what it cost him. "Good friends are hard to come by."

"Amen to that." She squeezed gently before releasing his hand. Brooke chose that moment to amble up, wrap Honor in a hug and thank her for coming. The rest of his sisters followed suit and circled around her, leaving him odd man out. They spoke of handbags, shoes and promises to hit the mall.

"I've had such a good time," Honor called out as she backed away. "Brooke, you have a blissfully happy marriage, okay?"

"That's the plan," Brooke answered, shimmering with happiness. Kids squealed in the background as they raced through the sprinkler, conversations from the deck rose and fell with the wind and his heart broke as he watched her walk away.

Friends, she said. Making it clear. He hadn't known how very much he'd been hoping until this moment. Until he knew anything more serious between them was an impossibility. He really ought to see her to her car, but his feet were rooted to the ground.

"She's easy to like," Colbie said at his side.

"Yeah. I know." He managed what he hoped passed for a grin, one that told his sister he was perfectly all right, no big deal, but he wasn't sure he pulled it off.

Across the green, Honor followed Jerrod through the French doors. She hesitated, glanced over her shoulder and their gazes connected. He read her appreciation and the apology in her eyes before she turned and walked out of his life.

Chapter Five

Luke McKaslin stayed on her mind during the long drive home. She broke her train of thought and the silence in her car by adding a few historical stories about Lewis and Clark's journey. A few signposts dotted the way, marking where the famous explorers had trekked. Jerrod nodded, listening, then plugged in his earbuds.

Maybe she had misread the caring thing, she reasoned as she waited for the Lamberts' wrought-iron gate to swing open at the end of the drive. When she'd mentioned the friendship thing, Luke had nodded as if that's all he'd felt. Just friendship, nothing more.

Good, she thought. The last thing she needed right now was a boyfriend. Or to hurt someone as nice as Luke who was hoping to be one.

"We're ten minutes late." Jerrod unbuckled before the car stopped rolling. He glanced at the front door as if waiting for his mother to burst out of it at any second. "She's gonna be peeved."

"You tell her it's my fault. I didn't want to speed." She kept an eye on the front door but no sign of Olive. "I'll see you bright and early in the morning for church?"

"I'll be there." The kid rolled his eyes. He might lack

enthusiasm, but at least he was grinning. "Thanks for taking me along."

"You had a good time?"

"I rocked at soccer."

"We both needed an outing big-time."

"No kidding." Jerrod heaved out of the car, shut the door and ambled up the front steps.

Her stomach rumbled as she motored onto the garage, a separate building with about ten bays, an extended carport off one side and rooms for employees above. Talk about a stellar day. The drive had been gorgeous, the reception had rocked and meeting Luke face-to-face, well, that had been a highlight. He'd felt like an old friend, as if she'd known him forever. Odd how that could happen.

She pulled into her space beneath the carport. *Thanks for this unexpected day,* she found herself praying. Only the good Lord knew how much she needed it. Once she'd felt isolated, but no more.

Maybe Montana wasn't that bad, she decided as she hopped out into the vibrant sunshine. Maybe it had been the loneliness that had gotten her down. Not that she'd ever actually like tromping through the woods or anything, and no way was she about to become an outdoors kind of person, but she felt happy. Really happy.

Her phone chimed, and joy leaped through her. Was it Luke? She had her cell out and squinted at the screen so fast, her hand was a blur. But it wasn't Luke. What did it say that it disappointed her?

How's it goin'? Kelsey's text read. U got mail.

She stopped, leaned against the side of the car and tapped in an answer. Uh oh. Good mail? Bad mail?

Job application mail.

Ominous, right? That could only mean one thing. Another rejection. She closed her eyes. Every door she tried to open employment-wise lately stayed firmly shut. She'd love to work at Wheatly again, but chances were good that wasn't going to happen anytime soon, not unless someone left their position or enrollment went back up. Given the present economy, not likely.

Which place? She asked.

La Jolla. Want me 2 open it 4 U?

Yes. Although she already knew what it would say. If the district had been interested in her, they would have called for an interview.

Sorry. They R not hiring.

No surprise. Her stomach tightened every time she thought about being unemployed again. While she may be counting down the days until she could zip home, she wasn't looking forward to her last paycheck.

How's things? she asked, pushing off the side of the car and popping the trunk. She gathered up her stuff, doing her best not to think about everything she liked about Luke.

Luke. She sighed. *Just stop thinking about the man, got it?* She closed her trunk, juggling purse, bag and phone, and dropped her keys. They clattered to the concrete and bounced to a stop beneath the car.

Of course.

Way to go, Honor. She set down her stuff, hunkered down on her knees and reached under the car. Her cell chimed with Kelsey's answer. It took a full minute of straining before the tips of her fingers caught the end of one of the keys and she could drag it out into the open.

When she looked up, a deer stood where the concrete met the grass, watching her with surprised button eyes.

Great. Now she was entertainment for the wildlife.

The phone chimed, the deer startled and leaped fluidly a few yards before stopping to watch.

It's not the same without U, Kelsey answered. I'll send an email with all the scoop. Going to a play tonight.

Give Anna Louise a hug 4 me.

Will do.

By the time Honor looked up, the doe had retreated to the edge of the lawn. She had to squint to make out the impression hidden in the grass. A little fawn, so sweet and delicate, curled up and napping, while his mama grazed.

Fine, so maybe Montana was starting to grow on her.

She marched up the stairs, unlocked her door and stumbled into her living quarters. Cool air washed over her as she opened the blinds. Windows looked out on the pristine forest and emerald hills and the doe grazing below.

A knock rapped on her door. It was Wren, dark-haired and a little plump, one of the downstairs maids.

"I brought you this." She held two covered plates and offered one. "I figured you didn't want to bother with Olive's drama. Mr. Lambert called. She's up in arms because he wants this house, too."

"See? Romance is a bad idea." She took the plate

with thanks. "Broken vows, broken relationships, div-vying up the property. Who needs to go through that?"

"Yep, we're smart to avoid it," Wren agreed with a wink. "But I keep telling myself, there has to be some good men out there. Finding them is the trick."

"You said it." Why Luke's face flashed into her mind was no mystery. He was a good guy.

Good guy. Wrong time.

"I'm going to go put my feet up, stare at the TV and do absolutely nothing while I eat an entire bag of bar-becue chips." Wren turned, heading next door.

"Hmm, a bag of chips. Great idea."

"You know it!" Wren's keys rattled, her door opened and she was gone.

Honor took her plate to the eating nook. Bless Wren, who knew how to make a sandwich. Cream cheese and sprouts spilled over the crusts, thick with tomato and turkey. Yum. Her stomach rumbled in anticipation.

Barbecue chips sounded good, so she shot over to the pantry. A strange sound in the apartment stopped her. Weird, because the strange sound was her. She was humming.

Actually humming. What could have prompted that? She snared the chip bag from the pantry, dropped into her chair, bowed her head to say grace and Luke's face flashed behind her eyelids. That man's friendship—not any deeper feelings—seemed to be the reason for her humming.

Lord, thank You for this day and for this meal. Thank You for new friends who have brightened my day. Amen. She raised her head and her cell chimed. She ripped open the chip bag and munched on a few chips while hunting down her phone. "Hello?"

"Good time or bad time?" Luke asked warmly.

"Any time is a good time." She couldn't deny it. The sound of his voice made the evening shine. "I'm surprised to hear from you, though. I'm guessing you would be busy with cleanup, knowing you."

"Yep, I just finished up. I wanted to give you a heads-up."

"Really? About what?" She made a beeline to the fridge and chose a can of cream soda.

"My sisters sure like you."

"I like them, too." She popped the top, guessing Luke was in his truck. She could hear the rush of the air-conditioning and the click, click of his turn signal.

"According to rumor, Brooke just sent you an email inviting you along on some plan of theirs. You can turn them down. You won't hurt any feelings."

"Why would I want to turn them down?"

"You haven't figured that out by now? After all those comments?"

"Oh, right, about me being your date." She plopped into a chair and grabbed the chip bag. "Sorry, I'm going to crunch in your ear, but I have a severe addiction to Ruffles."

"Can't blame you there."

Why was it always so easy to talk with Luke? From the very beginning, when she'd first read his comment on Good Books, she'd typed out a response as naturally as breathing.

Maybe that was proof this wasn't a romantic thing. Romance was a disaster—all those nerves, those silences that slipped into a conversation and a coiled-up stomach from being vulnerable. Friendship was much, much better.

"I just swung through the drive-thru," he confessed as something crackled in the background. "Since I couldn't resist Mr. Paco's Tacos, I might crunch a bit, too."

"Then at least we'll be crunching together." She hit speaker, so she had her hands free. "Don't worry about your sisters. I can set them straight on our friendship. What did they invite me to, do you know?"

"My guess is their volleyball team. They are down one member since that fiasco last week."

"Fiasco?"

"A sprained wrist. I wasn't there, but I heard it happened in the middle of a heated game."

"Where were you?"

"Where I always am." He paused to crunch into what sounded like a hard shell taco. "Taking care of my girls."

"Your cows." She loved that he called them that.

"I'm sweet on them, but don't you tell 'em. Once a female knows she has a man's heart, she has the upper hand."

"Is that right?"

"I don't want the whole herd to think they've got me wrapped around their hooves. I've got to maintain some semblance of control."

"It's a matter of pride."

"Glad you understand. I've got to hold on to as much of it as I can."

How was it possible that it felt like he was in the room with her, as if no distance separated them?

That's how you know this is just friendship, she thought. Because it had never been like this with one single man she'd ever dated. Luke was so simple to talk to. They had an effortless connection and natural accord. They simply got along, no fuss, no worries or those little insecurities that had always plagued her in a romantic relationship.

Wasn't this totally better?

Thank You, Lord, she sent up in prayer. *Thank You for friends and Montana cowboys.*

"You have to keep in mind I'm outnumbered, five hundred to one—well, two, if you want to count my brother, which I don't." His good-natured quip put a smile on her face, making it hard to bite into her sandwich.

"Poor Hunter. He didn't seem so bad when I met him. I was expecting a really dour, stern man, but he looked nice."

"It was an anomaly. An unexplained occurrence."

"Sure." Like she believed that. The ribbing between brothers was based on love and respect, and no amount of Luke's denial could disguise it from her. As their conversation continued and Luke began a funny story about his favorite cow, Betty, she took a bite of her sandwich, listening with all of her heart.

This was exactly what she needed in her life right now. A good buddy, someone to hang with and someone who wasn't looking for more.

The ranch came into view around the last corner in the country road. A sign their conversation had to end. Work awaited him and so did Hunter.

"I was surprised at your volleyball skills," she admitted, her gentle alto keeping his attention as he slowed for the turn up the hilly drive. "You never mentioned you were such a good player."

"When I joined the church in high school, the youth group was big into volleyball."

"So you've been playing a long time."

"More years than I'd care to admit." That was so long ago, another lifetime away. A painful time in his life when their dad had abandoned them and their mom had fallen apart. Mom hadn't made it for Brooke's wedding. That hurt, and he hoped the impact hadn't hit Brooke too hard. No one had raised their hopes very high but, still, it would have been nice if Mom had made the effort. "One day I dragged Hunter and Brooke along. Speaking of Hunter, guess who I see?"

"Your brother. You must be home." Did she sound a little sad about that?

"Almost." He was, too. He motored up the bumpy gravel drive, wanting to prolong the discussion. He didn't want to say goodbye. Two houses stood on the hill, an acre apart. The gray clapboard was his, the brown one at the end of the land was Hunter's. But where was his brother standing? On Luke's porch, hands on his hips, scowling.

"Looks like I'm in trouble." No surprise there. He circled into his drive and cut the engine. "I hate to say it, but I gotta go."

"Wow, time whizzed by. It's seven o'clock already. Give the calves a pat from me, oh, and Nell, too."

"Will do." He couldn't say goodbye. The word stuck on his tongue, refusing to be said. That wasn't a good sign, either. "Have a good night, Honor."

"You, too."

Sadness kicked through him when he ended the call. *You're in big trouble,* he told himself. *Big, big trouble.* He pulled the hand brake and hopped out into the hot summer evening. A dry wind whipped his face.

"You were talking with her, weren't you?" Hunter strode across the lawn. "She's going to make you sorry you ever typed 'howdy' to her."

"She's a nice lady." He joined his brother striding across the gravel to meet him. "Even you have to admit she's nice."

"I never said she wasn't. Everyone likes her."

"Then what's the problem?" He couldn't help teasing, as it was a younger brother's responsibility. "You don't have to look for doom."

"Someone has to." A grin twitched at the corners of his mouth. "I would have thought the doom was obvious."

"Don't know what you're talking about." Luke jiggled his keys as he tromped across the grass. "Nothing's going to go wrong between Honor and me. We're just friends."

That word was like a dagger in the chest, but no one needed to know.

"Just friends. Sure. Like I believe that." Hunter shook his head, dark hair tousled by the wind. "I saw the way you looked at her. You're smitten."

"Smitten? I don't think so." That wasn't a lie, considering what he felt was too powerful to be considered merely smitten. He'd describe it as stronger than full-blown like but shy of head-over-heels in love.

Good thing. He had a chance to put the brakes on his feelings before they got any more serious and before he got hurt.

"She's here for three more weeks." He actually said that as if it didn't hurt. "She'll go back to her life in California. I doubt she'll have time to hang out online, so don't get your suspenders in a knot."

"I'm not wearing suspenders." Hunter almost smiled. "I'm worried about you. A woman like that…well, I don't want you getting your hopes up."

"No worries. My hopes are right where they belong.

On the ground." He loped up the front steps. Harry, the cat curled up on the porch rail, watched him through slitted eyes.

"Good. When it comes to women, a man has got to be sensible."

"Is that why you haven't dated in the last decade?" Luke grabbed his barn boots from their spot by the front door. He swung around and sat on the top step to put them on.

"Yep. I'm the smart one. I keep women at a distance."

"I thought they were the ones staying away from you," he quipped.

"Either way works."

Luke shook his head. No idea what he was going to do with his brother. Hunter's heart had been broken real good long ago. He never recovered. Millie Wilson had been the love of Hunter's life. Some things a heart couldn't recover from.

Which was why he was glad he'd met Honor in person today. He'd seen it for himself. She wasn't interested in him. So he would stop hoping for more. They would stay friends, and only friends. End of story. There could never be anything more.

"Tomorrow I'm going to let the cows out here to graze." Hunter led the way across the lawn to the barn down the hill. "They'll get rid of these weeds. Better than using some chemical. Someone's got to go ride the irrigation lines before tonight's watering. I'm sure there's a leak in the pipes somewhere. Got to figure out where. Might as well have you do it."

"Me?" Amused, Luke squinted against the lowering rays of the sun, listened to the larks and robins singing in the pasture and stopped to wait for the old herd dog to lope up to him. He gave Nell a scrub on the head. "I might have important things to do with my evening."

"Doesn't matter. Besides, it might get your mind off your *friend* for a few hours."

"I thought we settled this. Honor can't break my heart."

"That's where you're wrong. She's a land mine. I've stepped on one just like that, and I'm trying to save you from it." Hunter winked, untied his horse's reins and swung up. "Don't forget I've got your back."

"With a brother like you, who needs enemies?" Luke quipped, chuckling, trying to pretend he didn't understand what Hunter was trying to do. He couldn't say his brother was wrong.

His heart was already a little broken over Honor Crosby. It would likely break more by the time their friendship was done.

The instant he set foot inside the barn, a symphony of calves mooing and lowing greeted him, scolding him for being late. His boots clomped on the cement as he called out a hello to his girls. The sun shone in the open doors and sifted through the breaks beneath the eaves, exposing bits of hay dancing in the air. Behind the barred gate, the herd watched him with friendly, long-lashed eyes, talking to him in their way, wanting attention like all God's creatures did.

"Ladies, I didn't mean to keep you waiting." He stopped to rub a nose here and a poll there. "I'll get your grain ready."

This was his life. There had to be a lady out there who could fit into it, a Montana girl who loved animals and ranch living. But honestly, it hurt to think about whoever she might be because he kept seeing Honor's face.

* * *

"Jerrod, this is very good." In the sunlit library, Honor looked up from reading his essay on Hemingway's book. "You supported your hypothesis perfectly, and your analysis of theme was top-notch. Well done."

"Thanks." Jerrod blushed at her praise, his math book open in front of him. His work papers littered the table near the window of walls that looked out at the summery deck and forest.

The work week was whizzing by since their weekend outing to Brooke's wedding, five days ago. Honor felt cheerful because she was about to see the McKaslins again.

And Luke.

Ignore that little leap, she told herself, laying a hand over her sternum. And focus on your job.

"How are the word problems coming along?" she asked.

"Slow, but I think I figured this one out."

"Good. I gave you some tough ones. Think of them as mental exercise."

"I'd rather do push-ups." Jerrod grinned.

She set aside his essay, unable to keep her gaze from sliding over to her laptop screen. Luke's most recent email stared at her.

Are you coming? Brooke wants to know, since she's the captain of the team.

Why isn't Brooke on her honeymoon yet? she typed and hit Send.

Because their cruise isn't booked until next month when she can get away from her job, came his reply.

And I'm only filling in for tonight?

That's the word. The player who injured her wrist will be back in two weeks.

Awesome. Tell Brooke I'm there as long as I don't get behind a truck carrying a big concrete tube thing again.

I'll relay the message. Looking forward to hanging with you tonight. Should be fun.

Definitely. Her face felt unusually warm, which made her realize she was humming again. Jerrod looked up from his work, clearly she'd interrupted him.

"Sorry, go back to work. Didn't mean to interrupt you." She ignored the teen's eye roll, glad to be happy again.

She had Luke to thank for that.

Chapter Six

"I didn't know you were so into volleyball." Colbie jogged up, the grass crunching beneath her feet. Dappled shadows from the overhead trees dotted her as she skidded to a stop. "This is the first time you've come to one of our matches."

"I'm starting to be a volleyball enthusiast." Shy about his feelings and hoping they didn't show, he dug a water bottle out of the cooler and handed it to her.

"You are so not fooling me, brother dear." She twisted off the cap and took a long pull. Behind her, other players were breaking up, seeking out cool drinks and towels after the first explosive set of the contest. "Any word from Honor?"

"Just that she got behind a gigantic tractor creeping down the highway and she'll be here when she can." He resisted the urge to haul out his phone and double-check the message she'd sent over a thirty minutes ago.

"It's a long drive just to come for a game. She must really like volleyball." Colbie took another swig.

"No comment." Really, how many times did he have to explain it to his sisters? At this point they weren't believing a thing he said.

"Who are we talkin' about?" Brooke hopped up, gladly taking the water bottle he handed her.

"Guess?" Colbie waggled her brows.

"Honor." Now Bree stumbled up, eager to join in the discussion. "I can't believe you talked me into taking her place until she gets here. I'm a disaster. Did you see my attempt at a serve?"

"Hey, you only hit the net twice."

"I'm a disgrace to the team. It's embarrassing."

"It really is," Colbie and Brooke teased.

Lots of people out tonight, even in the blazing summer heat. He scanned the park, watching for her. Sweat beaded his forehead so he swept off his Stetson. "Bree, where's Mac?"

"He pulled an evening shift otherwise I would be with him and wouldn't be here humiliating myself." Bree gave Colbie an affectionate nudge with her elbow. "I have a hard time saying no to you."

"And I used it to my advantage." Colbie dumped the remaining water over her head. "You're as red as a beet."

"Gee, thanks."

"No, I mean you need to hydrate." Colbie held out her hand, and Luke slapped a cold water bottle into it. "Drink up."

"There she is." Hardly paying attention to his sisters, he launched off the picnic table, striding into the scorching evening sun.

I'm just glad to see her, that's all, he told himself as he cut around a knot of volleyball players collapsed on the grass. It was a long drive, and he'd been worried. Anything could happen—an overheated engine, a leaking tire, a collision. It wasn't because his heart beat slower when he caught a glimpse of her welcoming smile. Nope, that wasn't the reason. Not even a little bit.

Maybe, if he tried hard enough, he could talk himself into believing it.

"Has the match started?" She rushed toward him, with the wide expanse of green lawn and Frisbee players between them. He couldn't hear her voice, but he could read her lips.

He nodded, hardly aware of his feet on the ground as he dodged a dog barreling after a tennis ball. "They took a break because of the heat."

"Over a hundred degrees." She dodged a Frisbee and suddenly she was before him, her long golden hair gleaming in the sun, her smile of welcome lighting him up. "Aren't you melting?"

"I came straight from the milking parlor." He hadn't taken time to change out of jeans and a T-shirt, although shorts and a tank would have been cooler.

She looked effortlessly beautiful in a teal tank edged with lace and simple denim shorts. Flip-flops snapped against her heels as she fell into stride beside him.

"You made good time considering the tractor."

"Thanks to a daring passing maneuver that I have to say was really impressive. I had to, because there I was creeping along at fifteen miles an hour. At that rate, by the time I actually showed, it would have been too late. Everyone would have finished up and gone home."

"I would have waited for you." It was easy to keep his tone light. Just friends.

"Good to know for next time."

"So you plan on making the trip again?"

"I'm negotiating for the entire day off Sunday, so I can attend the service here. Colbie's idea. *If* I show up on time and if you wouldn't mind the company?"

"I could probably be talked into it."

"Good. I was wondering who took my place on the team." Honor gestured toward the game, which had resumed. "I owe Bree big-time for filling in for me."

Bree chose that moment to turn around, spot Honor and wave. Colbie turned to see what had distracted Bree and waved, too. Brooke, getting ready to serve, cast her sisters a frowning look. "Honestly, you two, pay attention."

"But it's Honor!" Bree clasped her hands together. "You made it. Thank you! Come take my place."

"Okay, as you look desperate."

"I am! Save me."

Honor dove onto a spare corner of a picnic table bench, kicked off her flip-flops and dug out socks and athletic shoes from the big bag around her shoulder. On the field, Brooke pounded the ball, it streaked expertly over the net, the opposing church team scrambled but missed. He hardly noticed. Honor bounded up from the bench and shoved her things at him. "You look like the keeper of the stuff."

"Glad I'm useful for something." He took her bag. "Have fun."

"Oh, I intend to. Poor Bree." She loped off, unaware she left him standing alone with an emptiness he refused to examine. The women embraced, Honor trotted over to fill in the empty space alongside Brooke and Bree punched the air, victorious.

"I love to play, but honestly, I'm so not that good." Bree bounced toward him, long blond ponytail swinging. She reminded him of the girl she used to be, bright and sparkling and funny. That was before the armed robbery in the restaurant she'd worked at, when she'd been nearly fatally shot. She'd survived, but the ordeal had left its mark. Ever since the trial, where the gunmen were found guilty, she'd become more and more herself.

Lord, I thank You for that healing. It heartened him to see her skipping toward him. "I didn't think you were so bad."

"Ha! I'm alright in a family game, but some of these women could be pros. Yikes. Besides, look at Brooke. She rocks."

Their sister leaped at that moment, aggressively hammering the ball over the net. Another score. Her team cheered. He couldn't help watching Honor who high-fived Brooke and took possession of the ball, one-handed.

"Oh, she's good, too." Bree fell in beside him, leaning against the picnic table as Honor's serve rocketed through the air. "I noticed that when we played at the reception. Do you think there's a chance she'll stick around when her job is over?"

"Nope. Not the slightest." If he were far from home, missing those he was closest to, he wouldn't stay around a second longer than necessary. Not unless he had strong feelings for someone.

But face it, he was the only one with strong feelings.

"That's too bad. I like her." Bree gave her ponytail a toss and lifted her face toward the sun, drinking in its brightness. "I think she likes you, too."

"Sure. We're great friends." For the ten billionth time.

"Oh, I don't know about that. She drove two hours to see you."

"Because she misses her friends back home and she's lonely. Can't blame her there."

"I don't think that's the whole story. Whatever the reason, she's *here*. Make the most of it." Bree jabbed him affectionately with her elbow. "You're a good catch, Luke. Trust me. She's looking at you."

Sure, he knew that, since his heart stopped beating. He sent Honor a crooked grin, one he hoped said, hey there, friend.

She smiled back to him the same way. Not that his hopes were up, he was too practical for that. But a little piece of hope tumbled, anyway, disappointed.

You've got to stop dreamin', buddy, he told himself as Colbie shouted Honor's name. Her head whipped back to the game and she jumped, sending the ball streaking over the net for another score.

"Whew, all this fun is addictive." Honor accepted the water bottle Luke handed her. "I could do more of this."

"Great," Brooke spoke up. "I'll keep you in mind if Terry's wrist isn't better by next week."

"You should hang with us more often," Bree added. "We know how to have lots of fun."

"I've noticed." It was nice being wanted and she adored the McKaslin sisters. Honestly, what wasn't to like? "You all have brightened things up for me lately."

"Then maybe you want to hang around now that the match is over and adequately won." Colbie rubbed a towel over her damp head. "We're heading over to the bakery."

"Brandi's working tonight," Luke managed to get a word in edgewise as he secured the lid on the cooler. "She was the smart one."

"Yeah, staying in the air-conditioning," Brooke agreed, heading toward the parking lot. "Smart."

"Brilliant, as I'm melting." Bree pressed the cold water bottle against her forehead. "I'm thinking an iced mocha and a big scoop of ice cream."

"Ooh, I'm thinking two scoops." Brooke led the way toward the parking lot. "You're coming, right, Honor?"

"I came all this way. I might as well make the most of it." As the sisters' voiced their pleasure, she caught Luke's eye. The warmth of his smile made her palms go damp.

Or, maybe that was just the hundred-plus temps. Yes, that was probably it.

"You can follow me if you want." Luke sidled in as the sisters broke apart, each heading for their own vehicles. "Or you can ride with me, and I'll bring you back to your car."

"Ride with him," Colbie called as she unlocked her SUV. "It'll be easier finding the highway north from here. Once you get into downtown, it's a little confusing."

"I guess that settles it." She left her keys in her purse and headed toward Luke's shining white pickup.

"Great. See ya there!" Colbie bobbed into her vehicle. Bree tooted her horn as she backed out of her spot. Brooke waved as she waited for Bree to drive off so she could back up.

"Guess you're stuck with me." Luke opened the door for her.

"I think I can survive it." She hopped onto the seat. Those dimples of his were absolutely to die for. Did he know how handsome he was? The bigger question was, why hadn't some woman snatched him up?

"Good. How's Jerrod doing?"

"He's doing okay, considering the last thing a teenage boy wants to do with his summer is study for a test he doesn't want to take." She hadn't driven like a madwoman for one hundred and thirty-eight miles to bore him with the details. "How are your girls?"

"My cows are nothing but trouble. It's all I can do to keep the upper hand."

"I'm so not fooled." Why her eyeballs drifted downward to study his steel shoulders was a complete mystery. "You have them in the palm of your hand."

"They are sweet on me."

I'm sure, she thought. Muscles rippled under his white T-shirt as he closed her door and circled in front of the truck. Who wouldn't be sweet on him?

She certainly wasn't.

Luke's door yanked open, he hopped in and plugged his key in the ignition. "I can't imagine having a different job or living a different life."

"It suits you. Did you always know you wanted to run a dairy?"

"I wanted to own my land and make a living raising animals. I grew up on a cattle ranch and I loved trailing my dad around. When he actually worked, that is." He checked his mirrors, waiting for another car to pull out first. "It's the only life I've ever wanted."

"It's a blessing to do what you love for a living." She pulled down the visor to block the sun and caught her reflection in the mirror. Yikes.

"After I graduated high school, Hunter got me a job working for Wilson's Dairy, just around the corner from where we are now." The coast was clear, so he angled the truck out of its spot. "We worked ten years saving every penny until we could come up with a down payment for our place."

"You're a Montana man through and through."

"You know it." The truck lumbered through the lot. "So, how about you? Did you always know you wanted to be a teacher?"

"No. When I was little I wanted to be a princess."

She finger combed her hair, but it wouldn't stop sticking straight up. Figures. "I was taken in by the tiara thing. Then I wanted to be a ballerina. It was the tutu, so frilly and pink, but those things didn't work out for some reason."

"Imagine that." He hit the blinker and turned onto the street.

"When I hit kindergarten, I became much more practical. I wanted to work with Big Bird."

"Who wouldn't?"

"In high school, I volunteered for a program that helped kids with challenges with their homework. I was paired up with a seventh grader who was struggling with remedial reading, and that experience changed my life. I pray that I changed hers, too."

"I'm sure you did."

"It was rewarding and I was hooked. My parents wanted me to go into something more lucrative, but I refused. Life isn't about how much money you make."

"Amen to that." He eased his foot off the gas, slowing at a red light. "Do you have anything lined up next?"

"I'm still putting in applications, but it's tough competition with so many cutbacks. I'll probably wind up substituting next year."

"Have you thought about moving out of the area? Maybe someplace outside of L.A.?"

"No. I'm not that desperate. Yet." The light changed, the truck accelerated through the intersection and she couldn't help thinking that if she needed anymore confirmation, this was proof enough. She and Luke were two very different people, wanting different things in life.

"Jerrod is a good kid," Luke said. "You must like teaching him."

"I do. He's going through a tough time, so I understand. My parents divorced when I was his age. They get along all right now and have remarried. But it was rocky for a while."

"Been there. My dad left when I was a kid. Tough times, watching our family come apart. He cheated on Mom. He cheated on us."

"It affects you."

"It does. That's why I'm leery of females."

"Even me?"

"Especially you." A dash of humor sparkled in his eyes. "You are big trouble."

"The biggest," she agreed. "The truth is, when you see a marriage come apart, you look at romance differently after that."

"You know it can end. That if you put your faith in someone, they let you down completely."

Honor remembered something Brooke had said. That Luke's last girlfriend had led him on and then let him down.

"That's why I'm single." He hit his blinker and turned left. "You wouldn't want to date me, not that you're interested. I break hearts right and left."

"Sure, I noticed that right off. Me, too, by the way. I leave a long string of broke hearts behind me wherever I go." Not even close to the truth. And Luke was too kind to ever have broken anyone's heart. To ever let anyone down intentionally at all.

It was very hard not to like that.

After two more quick turns, Luke pulled into a large parking lot rimmed by stores. One of them was an adorable bakery with a striped awning and a long front wall of glass.

"Honor!" Her door was wrenched open the moment

the truck stopped. Bree grinned up at her, platnium hair dancing in the wind. "I hope you like chocolate."

"Like it? Oh, no, like is too mild of a word." She took a moment to soak in one last sight of Luke's grin before grabbing her bag and hopping to the blacktop. "Love? Still too mild. It's an obsession, at least. Maybe an addiction?"

"Me, too!" Bree took her hand.

"Me, three!" Colbie took her other hand.

"I'm not going to say me, four. That's just too cheesy." Brooke shut the truck door and the group of them arrowed straight toward the bakery.

How fun was this? She glanced over her shoulder at the man bringing up the rear. Luke shrugged back, slipping his truck keys in his jeans pocket. What a handsome picture he made with his rugged good looks, athletic gait and easy going kindness.

That's not my heart swooping, she told herself firmly. She had no interest in going through the wringer of romance anytime soon. What were the chances what she felt was heartburn?

"You've got to have the triple chocolate, chocolate chip cupcake." Bree opened the door.

"It's to die for," Colbie agreed, tugging her into the shop. Honor stumbled after her, breathing in the aroma of an amazing condition of sugar, chocolate, cinnamon and a whiff of hazelnut as she approached the glass case.

Everything delicious stared back at her—glazed pastries, frosted cinnamon rolls, colorfully decorated cookies and cupcakes with funny icing faces.

"Hey!" Brandi sauntered up to the counter in a yellow T-shirt, jeans and a ruffly apron. "How did the game go? You all look victorious."

"That's cuz we are." Colbie punched the air. "At the last minute."

"Due to me," Bree admitted. "I was the weak link."

"Weak? How about the worst?" Brooke lovingly wrapped an arm around Bree's shoulder. "But we were glad to have you on the starting lineup. It was a lot of fun, right?"

"Oh, tons of fun." Bree shook her head, mouthing, *not fun*. "But sadly now that you have Honor, I'll just have to stay on the sidelines."

"Or not even show up at all." Brandi waggled her eyebrows. "Am I smart, or what?"

"Waaay smart," Bree agreed and the twins laughed, two peas in a pod. Nothing could be cuter.

This is what I've been missing, Honor realized. The bond of friends and the fun of sisters. Home seemed a million miles away.

"We'll have five triple chocolate monster cupcakes." Colbie pointed at the display case. "With big scoops of lavender ice cream. I don't know about you all, but I'm having an iced mocha."

"Me, too," Honor spoke up, eyeing the size of the cupcakes. She would have to take up jogging to burn off all those calories, but nothing had ever looked more indulgent.

"My treat." Luke sidled up next to her, pulling out his wallet.

There went that funny feeling in her chest again, but it would be smart to keep on denying it. There were too many reasons why Luke McKaslin could not be anything more than a friend.

Chapter Seven

"...**a**nd then Luke climbed back down the tree." Colbie scraped the bowl with her spoon for the last of the ice cream.

"Climbed? I slid more than climbed and then I fell." He polished off his iced decaf latte. "It was humiliating. I looked like an idiot."

"A heroic idiot," Brooke corrected affectionately. "You were such a good guy going up there to rescue Fluffy."

He shook his head, wishing he could shake away the conversation as easily. But nothing would stop his sisters from extolling what they thought of as his virtues in front of Honor. Rescuing Colbie's neighbor's newly adopted cat was apparently one of them. All because he hadn't been able to take Madge's worried sobs as she gazed up at her kitty in the high branches of the maple.

"It was nothing." He shrugged, aware of Honor across the table, watching him with a curious look on her face. Probably thinking he was a sentimental sap. He'd always been a softy. It wasn't a quality that had single women lining up to run after him. He straightened his shoulders and cleared his voice, hoping to sound tougher. "How is the cat doing?"

"Fine. He wasn't the one who hit the ground on his back after an eight-foot fall." Brooke just had to say it, didn't she? "Honor, Luke did it on purpose. I watched him twist in midair so that he would land hard and keep Fluffy safe in his arms."

Honestly. Heat stained his face. Could his sister be anymore obvious? A while ago, he never should have admitted to her he was sweet on a lady he'd met on-line. No doubt, Brooke figured out he'd meant Honor.

If only he could derail the conversation. His efforts didn't seem to work, but he couldn't let that stop him from keeping at it. Persistence was the key to most successes. "Is Fluffy adjusting to life with Madge?"

"The bigger question here is you." Concern crinkled Honor's unguarded blue eyes. "Were you hurt?"

"Nothing that didn't heal." More heat burned his face.

"Don't believe him for a second." Brooke looked determined to set the record straight. "He cracked a rib—"

"Why didn't you write me about that?" Honor asked, her confusion in her eyes getting to him.

"—he got a mild concussion when his head hit the patio," Colbie added.

"He was bruised from head to toe from the impact," Bree chimed in.

"Not to mention scratched to smithereens thanks to Fluffy's claws." Brandi stopped by with a water pitcher in hand and leaned in to refill glasses. "He was a sight."

"It wasn't that bad. Or at least it didn't seem that way." He took a pull from his newly filled water glass. "I healed up. Brooke, you never answered me about Madge—"

"When did this happen?" Honor interrupted him, her gentle concern hitting him harder than any blow. Worry pinched her beautiful face. There was nothing more lovely than seeing her concern for him.

And her disappointment. He knew what she would say next. "Last month," he admitted.

"We were emailing every day. You didn't think to tell me?" Ever gentle, but reprimand steeled her words.

"It was no big deal." His chest tightened up, realizing his sisters had gone silent and Brandi watched him carefully as she circled the table, pouring water. He swallowed only to find his throat felt like it had fifty pebbles stuck in it. How did he explain he'd been afraid of sounding like a fool? In his view, it was no way to impress a city girl like Honor. "I healed up, but I'm not sure about Fluffy. I think I traumatized him. Every time he sees me, he takes off and hides."

"Even when he's sitting in the windowsill," Colbie added. "Madge says Fluffy dives behind the couch every time Luke pulls up in his truck."

"Smart cat." Brandi set aside the pitcher and began stacking empty plates and bowls. "He's a sweetie, though. Long fluffy hair. Very snuggly."

"I'm glad Madge adopted a pet. She seems happier with him around." Brooke began stacking dishes, helping out. "It's kind of quiet here tonight."

"Quiet? It's dead." Brandi gestured to the span of empty tables. The few other customers had left and no one else had arrived. "Things have been getting slower and slower. I wasn't going to mention this until later, but Ava is cutting back shop hours."

"Oh, no. I was afraid of that." Bree shook her head, scattering long blond locks. "That means fewer hours for us."

"A lot fewer." Brandi's chin went up as if it didn't bother her a bit.

He wasn't fooled. He knew how tight the twins' budgets were, both still in college.

"I know that look." Colbie spoke up. "There's more bad news, isn't there?"

"All right. It gets worse," Brandi admitted. "Business is down so much, Ava can't keep both of us on. Not only will hours be cut, but one of us has to go."

"That is bad news." Luke knew what this meant. The girls were self-supporting. There was no help coming in from Dad or from their mother, who struggled with her own issues. Added to dwindling financial aid and rising college tuition, he worried they wouldn't be able to complete their education. "What about your last semester?"

"I don't know." Brandi shrugged.

Bree hung her head for a moment, then straightened her shoulders. "We'll work it out."

"I could always use help on the ranch." He and Hunter made hiring decisions together, but he knew Hunter would agree. "We're short a field hand for haying. We start cutting tomorrow."

"I'm in." Brandi spoke over the top of her twin. "No arguments. Rent will be due before we know it and so will our tuition—"

"But you love working here." Bree spoke louder, drowning out Brandi's protests. "I wouldn't mind learning to drive a tractor."

"No way!" Brandi swirled away, loaded down with plates. "It's already decided, right, Luke?"

"Uh—" He shook his head, liking the way Honor smiled at him.

"You're not in charge," she told him, amused.

"Apparently not." He watched Bree leap from the

table to follow her twin, the two talking rapidly, and disappear into the kitchen. "I wonder who will win?"

"Brandi," Brooke decided.

"She doesn't have a fiancé in town. Bree should stay here close to Mac," Colbie agreed. "Well, I've totally destroyed my calorie quota for the day."

"Me, too." Honor didn't seem too bummed about it.

"Me, three." Brooke tried to smile, but Luke knew she was worried about the twins. The three of them shared an apartment not far from campus before Brooke got married.

He was worried, too. The seasonal work that he could offer Brandi would only be a short-term solution. Maybe he and Hunter could instigate a little private scholarship help. Their funds were tight, too, but surely they could dig up something to contribute. The girls needed to finish their degrees. It was as simple as that.

"Hey, you look worried." A hand landed on his forearm. A sense of peace rolled through him from the impact of Honor's touch. She'd taken Bree's abandoned chair next to him. Looking into her caring gaze, he saw a friend's concern.

Try not to let that get to you, he thought. *Don't let yourself wish it was more.*

"I was so excited to learn the twins are both going to be teachers." Honor stood, moving away, talking over the squeak of her chair and the clamor as Brooke and Colbie stood, too. "I hope they love it as much as I have."

Somewhere along the line he'd missed that conversation. The women talked, chatting pleasantly as they called out goodbyes to Brandi and Bree. Neither twin reappeared. That troubled him as he held the door for the ladies.

There they were, talking away again and he'd missed what they were saying.

"I think so, too." Honor looked happy about whatever it was. "Count me in."

"For what?" he asked as she brushed by him into the evening's long shadows. Cheerful sunlight peeked over the top of the roof, glaring into his eyes as he followed her along the sidewalk.

"Don't tell him. Let him guess." Colbie looked pleased as she ambled toward her SUV. "Honor, I'll email you."

"Let me give you my addy—"

"I already have it," Brooke interrupted. "I'll forward it to Colbie."

"Good deal." Honor waited by the truck. What a picture she made standing in the long streaks of the evening sun. It lit her up, highlighting her beauty.

He hit the remote and the locks popped. He opened the door to the sounds of the women's goodbyes, the rev of engines and the beep of horns as his sisters drove off. Which made him think of the twins still inside the bakery, worrying over their futures. He'd call Brandi as soon as he dropped off Honor.

"What are you and my sisters up to?" he asked.

"Nothing good." Her humor dazzled. She stepped into the truck, lost her balance and she grabbed his shoulder.

"See? I'm clumsy." She blushed, righted herself and tumbled onto the seat. "Usually at the worst possible time."

"At least I was here to catch you. Next time, who knows?"

"Right." Her head spun. She felt breathless. Did she really want to admit why? At least she had a chance to catch her breath when he closed the door, leaving her inside the truck alone. Alone to deal with how solid his shoulder had felt. Like granite. Immovable. Unshakable. Like the kind of man who never wavered.

I really don't want to see him as a man instead of a friend, she thought, tracking him as he crossed in front of the truck to the driver's side. His door opened and he swung in, his masculine strength and presence undeniable. Her stomach gave a tumble. That couldn't be a good sign.

"You seem to really get along with my sisters." He started the engine.

"They're great. I feel like I fit right in."

"And you've already agreed to do something with them. Shopping, probably, right?" He quirked a brow, looking dashing in a country strong kind of way. Golden good looks, boy-next-door honest. Hard to resist.

"Right." She buckled up, acting like a woman who wasn't noticing the man seated beside her. She was an unaffected woman. A woman made of steel. "Shopping."

"Should have known." Luke started the truck. "You women are going to hit the mall?"

"A girl's gotta shop."

"So I hear."

She leaned back against the cushiony seat, trying to focus on the scenery out the window—reaching blue sky, sunshine glinting off car windows and leafy trees lining the parking lot, but where did her eyes sneak to?

Luke. "You're troubled about the twins."

"I am." He wheeled down the street. "Not sure how easy it will be for them. They start student teaching in the fall."

"Which leaves little time for an outside job, since

it's a huge job in itself." She smiled, remembering that sweet time in her life. "When I was student teaching, I had a kind teacher who really believed in me. My students made it easy."

"What grade?"

"Eighth. I know that's a tough time for kids, but I love that age. Still part kid, not yet adult. It's the grade I used to teach."

"That had to be a hard job to lose."

"Very." That was what she liked about Luke. He understood. Always. "I miss it. It's really something to watch your students grow and change throughout the school year. To make a connection with them and to help them, through learning, to take another step toward becoming the adults they are meant to be."

"Sound like you're in the right profession." The way he gazed at her with a nod of approval and a gleam of appreciation made her warm inside. It was cozy, feeling as if she belonged right here, in this moment, with this man.

"You understand because that's how you feel about your work."

"I've worked with animals all my life. You don't put in that kind of commitment and hard work if you don't love it."

"And you never get tired of living in the middle of nowhere? Don't get me wrong. This is beautiful country, but it's remote."

"It's the way I grew up. It's all I've known." He shrugged. "Hey, I see that look."

"What look?"

"The appalled one. Bordering on horror."

"Not horror." Honestly. That man could make her

laugh. "More like shock. You have to drive almost an hour just to go to a movie."

"And after the movie, I have to be back before milking time." He eased to a stop at an intersection. "Cows have to be fed and milked on time. That's ranching life."

"So, matinees only?"

"It's not so bad." He chuckled, a warm, buttery sound that made the sunshine brighter. The light changed and he motored into the intersection. "I'm my own boss, except when Hunter thinks he's in charge. I get to work outdoors, unless I'm in the milking parlor. I like what I do. It's a good life. The benefits make up for the shortcomings."

"There are no jammed freeways. No smog. Not a crowd anywhere."

"The scenery is great. It's not the ocean, but it's great."

"It's a good fit for you here." She admired him for that. "You're the outdoor type. You would be unhappy, say, as a lawyer or an accountant. For instance, I can't imagine you working at my father's firm."

"Me, either." He hit the blinker and turned, and the green lawns of the park came into view.

A sinking feeling settled deep in her chest. Her time with Luke was almost over.

"I'm definitely not a suit-and-tie city guy, but that's okay. God's made a different path for each and every one of us."

"It's being true to that path and to Him that matters." There was her car, sitting in the shade. Aspens rustled as she opened the truck's door. Why didn't she want to leave?

"You're right about that."

She opened her door before he could move and slid

off the seat, landing on her feet. "Paths can get tricky, though. Sometimes you think you can see where you're going and then surprise. There's a dip in the road you couldn't see until you were right up on it."

"I don't know about you, but those dips tend to be tough."

"Agreed." Winding up in Montana, for instance. Just a dip in the road. Nothing permanent. Nothing but a pit stop on her journey. "But there are good dips, too."

"Wait a minute. You didn't just call me a dip, did you?"

"I'll never tell." She walked away to the sound of his amused laughter.

No doubt about it. She liked hanging out with Luke. She dug her keys out of her bag. "I'll see you on Good Books tomorrow night, right?"

"Count on it. I've got to hurry up and finish reading that blockbuster we're scheduled to talk about. I'm not even halfway."

"Slacker. I have two more chapters to go."

"Show off." Affection warmed his words, making them sound wonderful.

What was she going to do about that? She didn't know as she unlocked her car and settled behind the wheel. Luke waited until she had the engine started before he drove off with a tap of his horn and a tug on her heart.

Yes, she definitely liked that man.

She checked her phone, not surprised to find the text message Colbie had promised. I'll keep you up-to-date on Luke's birthday bash plans. Glad you're on board.

Me, too, she thought, buckled up and put her car in gear. Her cell rang a few seconds after she'd left the lot.

Turning onto the main road out of town, she slipped on her Bluetooth. "Hi, Kelsey."

"Hey, I got lonely for you so I had to call."

"What are you up to?" She trundled out of the city limits, where rolling meadows and farmland dominated.

"Sitting out by the pool. The apartment is lonely ever since my roommate took off for rural Montana."

"What was she thinking?" Honor joked, since she was the roommate. She definitely missed the small two-bedroom unit she shared with Kelsey. Their friendship stretched all the way back to college, where they'd been on the same dormitory floor freshman year. "If it's any consolation, I miss being there. I don't know how many times in an evening I look up from planning lessons to say something to you."

"I know. Old habit. I thought we'd share a place until one of us married. Worse, there are no single men in this complex."

"Sure there are single men. Look harder."

"Okay, there's the guy from building A, but he's such a player. I can hear him from across the pool trying to convince a new tenant that he used to be in Special Forces."

"Maybe in a video game. I know just the guy you are talking about. Big bunchy, muscled arms?"

"That's the one. Where are all the sincere guys? I think they went out of vogue somewhere in the last few decades and I'm protesting."

"I think there are men like that." Was it wrong that she immediately thought of Luke? As the road ribboned ahead of her through the waning sunshine, she couldn't help remembering how gentlemanly he was and how sincere. "I think the real problem might be they all live in Montana."

"Bummer. How could anyone move away from the beach?"

"Good question," she agreed, thinking of jogging along the ocean, watching the wide stretch of blue. There were sunny afternoons at the beach club and shore-side picnics with her friends. She drove toward the setting sun, missing her life in Malibu so sorely, her soul ached.

Chapter Eight

"What are you doin'? Reading again?" Hunter crunched across the lawn in his cowboy boots, laying his hand on a grazing cow's rump as he approached.

Betty lifted her head from grazing and mooed sweetly, long eyelashes batting. For a moment, Hunter's gruffness vanished and he tossed the bovine a grin as he passed.

On his porch swing, Luke closed his book. Hard to get any reading done with Hunter in the vicinity. "What are you doing over here? I thought you'd be putting up your feet for the evening. Morning comes early around here."

"And I'm doing the morning milking. Don't remind me." Hunter clomped up the steps, stopping to pet Harry, curled up on the porch rail. The cat purred rustily. "I just got off the phone with Brandi."

"Can she come tomorrow?"

"She'll be here bright and early. We need help, and the hay doesn't cut itself." Hunter leaned against a support post and crossed his arms over his chest. "What about you? Can I count on you?"

"Why the question? You know I can drive a tractor. We grew up on a ranch, haying every season." He knew his brother and he knew that look. "What's on your mind?"

"You're sweet on that city woman."

"Honor? That's a negatory." Sweet didn't come close to what he felt. And since his heart wasn't Hunter's business, Luke wasn't obligated to divulge any further information.

"You're hoping she'll stay in Montana, aren't you? I heard you whistling when you came home last night. I heard from Brandi she played volleyball with the girls."

"They were a player short and she's pretty good at it."

"I know you. You're going to get involved with her and get your heart broke when she leaves. Because she will leave."

"I appreciate the concern, Hunter. We're brothers. We've got to look out for each other."

"We've been doing it since we were small. I know trouble when I see it. Did you get a good look at her? Those shoes, that bag. She shouts expensive."

"I have eyes. I saw." The car she drove was probably worth three times what he'd paid for his pickup. She may be a schoolteacher, but she came from a family of means. "You can stop worrying, bro. I know how things are. So can we drop this?"

He loved his brother, he really did. Hunter remembered the devastation Sonya had left behind years ago. A big city girl spending time with him, letting him fall for her and finding out she'd never intended to stay. She'd just been using him so she wouldn't feel lonely. She'd been passing time, that was all. When she left town, she'd never looked back.

"Fine." Hunter pushed away from the post. "Your

mind will be on work and getting Brandi settled come morning? I'll be busy in the milking parlor."

"You know I will be." He checked his watch. The online book chat was about to start. Looked like he wouldn't get the last chapter finished in time. He climbed to his feet, gave Harry a scrub on the head and opened the door. Air-conditioning met him as his boots rang on the hardwood floor.

Nell lifted her chin off her paws to greet him sleepily. She lay on her bed by the couch, drowsing.

"Hey, girl. You've had a long day." He knelt to pet her. They had been friends for a long time. "Are you ready to ride in the tractor with me tomorrow? Or are you going to hang with Hunter?"

Nell perked her ears, interested, and tilted her head.

"Maybe you'll choose Brandi over both of us."

Nell panted, her eyes sparkling at Brandi's name.

"That's what I thought." He headed to the kitchen table where his laptop sat waiting. He plunked his unfinished book down beside it. It felt like his chest was tied in knots. He wished he could control how he felt.

He leaned back in his chair while his laptop started up and stared out the big bay window in the kitchen nook. His land spread out before him and he took pride in it, eyeing the barn, the green pastures where cows grazed and the fenced fields of growing hay waiting to be cut. Those fields stretched for a mile. Foothills rimmed the rural ranching valley, a river winked in the distance and mountains framed it all. An incredible view, one he got to enjoy every day.

He couldn't imagine living anywhere else and wouldn't want to. He was entrenched here. It wasn't as if he could pack up and move to, say, Malibu.

Luke? Are you there? A private message popped on his screen from California Girl.

I'm wishing I'd managed my time better since I didn't finish the book. I spent too much time yesterday with a certain pretty gal.

Not sure who that would be.

Me, either. Strange how his emotional connection to her strengthened every time they communicated. How did your day go?

Let's just say it was interesting.

Uh-oh. That doesn't sound good.

True. I have a few problems to solve. How was yours?

Busy. What kind of problems?

The future employment kind.

Still no job offer? He leaned back in his chair, picturing her at her computer. A crinkle of worry, the soft purse of her mouth and the self-conscious shrug of her slender shoulders when she wasn't sure if she wanted to open up or not.

Nope. With all the rejections I keep getting, it feels like I'm being blocked every which way I turn. I keep thinking, what are You trying to tell me, Lord? What am I missing?

Sounds frustrating.

More like a comedy of errors. Maybe I need to stop worrying about it and trust God has plans for me.

I wonder who gave you that advice over a month ago?

Let me think. Oh, right, it was you. Easy to picture her beautiful smile and hear the musical note of that little laugh she made. Tell me about your day.

I got home last night in time to help Hunter deliver a late season calf.

How sweet. Are mama and baby okay?

Just fine. The newborn is a cute little thing, mostly black with one white ear and one black ear and a white blaze down her nose.

Adorable.

It's my turn to come up with a name. Would you like to do it?

Would I! Let me think…

Let me describe her. Maybe that will help. She's a little bitty thing with big chocolate eyes and long lashes. A little star on her forehead

How about Faith?

I like it. Faith, it is.

Hey, there are a lot of upsides to your job. Baby cows, naming them, big brown eyes looking up at you adoringly.

Only because I've got the bottle.

I'd love to see that.

Seriously? I could invite you out sometime.

I'd like that. You know the chat has started without us.

I know, but I didn't finish the book.

Then I guess we can keep chatting. No sense joining into the discussion and have them give away the ending. It's a surprise. You'll want to discover it for yourself.

The next time Luke looked up, the sun had set, his reflection stared back at him in the black window and Nell was snoring.

Waaay past his bedtime. 4:00 a.m. came early in the morning, but did he want to break off their chat? Not a chance. He stayed at his computer much longer than he'd intended, the book discussion they'd missed was long over and he still couldn't bring himself to type goodnight no matter how many times he yawned. Honor brought light to his life he would never be able to replace when she was gone. In a little over two weeks she would be heading back to her life in California and she'd have little to no time to spend online with him.

It was good he spent time with her while he could.

Okay, it's ten-thirty and I really have to go.

Honor read Luke's words on her screen with a smile. They had been chatting online for over two hours. Her back hurt, her backside ached from the uncomfortable chair and her eyes were going blurry. You said that thirty minutes ago.

And I hope I mean it this time.

Because 4a.m. comes early?

Yes, it does. Every morning.

It was easy to picture him at his computer with his tousled sandy hair and his shy, lopsided grin. She could no longer deny the rather large flutter in her chest. She had a crush on the man. That was all. A tiny, hardly noticeable case of the isn't-he-greats.

Give Faith a pet from me, she tapped out on the keys. I've never named a calf before. I'm attached now.

Remember you're welcome to come meet her. Anytime.

I'll keep that in mind. Go. Get some sleep. We'll talk later.

And you can tell me how your job hunt goes.

It's a date. Ugg. Why had she used that word? She rolled her eyes.

Same time tomorrow?

Yes. Bye.

Good night, my friend.

Friend. Wasn't that a word she used to love to use in reference to him? A word that made her feel safe and accepted without any of that pesky, turmoil-ridden romance stuff.

Good night, friend. She typed back. A message popped onto the screen. Montana Cowboy has left.

Her heart fluttered again. Probably it was best to keep ignoring it. Likely as not, it would pass. No need to get concerned.

The silent room echoed around her as she checked her inbox, spotting the expected email from Colbie. She read the plans for Luke's birthday party as the shadows deepened. The little studio apartment turned dark. Nightfall came late this time of year, and she pushed away from the table to flick on lamps. She was closing the blinds when she spotted a movement in the courtyard below. Hard to ignore the bad feeling arrowing into her gut.

She leaned in for a closer look and recognized the figure hiking across the grounds. It couldn't be safe to hang out in the forest this time of night, right? She shivered, thinking of all the creepy crawly things as she headed out the door.

The warm night surrounded her as she hurried down the steps, her flip-flops snapping. Realizing too late she wasn't geared up for a trek in the woods, she almost turned around to fetch better shoes but the shadow in the distance stopped. He sat down on the ground and put his face in his hands.

The poor kid. She headed in his direction. His shoulders stiffened when he heard her coming. He swiped at his eyes, so she took her time so he could hide all evidence of his emotions before she sat down beside him.

"What's up?" The wild grasses crunched beneath her. Daisies bobbed in the dark shadow of the towering trees. She tried to sound casual, as if she hadn't notching his tears.

"Nothing much." He sounded stuffy. His voice bobbed up and down with the effort to sound casual. "Just needed to get out of the house. You know, get some fresh air."

"And commune with nature?"

"Yeah. Something like that." He stared into the dark shadows, where trees merged with the coming night.

"You had a long day today."

"I guess." His voice wobbled again, hiding something.

"Your mom is bound and determined to get you into Wheatly." *C'mon,* she thought. *Talk to me, Jerrod.*

He hung his head and said nothing. She sat there, waiting. The last dregs of light faded from the horizon, leaving them in near total darkness.

"I miss my dad." Jerrod's voice cracked. "I miss my friends back home."

"I know what you mean." She thought of Kelsey and Anna Louise, who were probably wrapping up their weekly beach picnic and bible study about now. "If I were home, I'd be hanging with my friends, sitting on the beach with a big bag of take-out hamburgers and fries. We'd be sharing our favorite Bible verses. Probably eating Anna Louise's cookies for dessert. She's a fantastic baker."

"I'd be surfing. Well, probably not right now, but I'd have been up early on my board."

"I miss the way the ocean smells."

"And the sound of the waves."

"The way they sweep on the shore and wipe the sand clean, the way God's grace can erase our mistakes."

"I miss the hot dog place near Surfrider Beach."

"Smoothies at the club." She longed for the soft feel of the chaise lounges, the slick of sunscreen on her skin and the company of her friends. Yoga class and wading in the ocean and hopping into the car, having anything she wanted to minutes away. "Do you know what I miss most?"

"Your friends."

"Bingo." Kelsey's laughter and Anna Louise always trying to feed them all. "Not that Montana is so bad. It's pretty in its own way."

"I liked it when Dad would bring us up here for a couple weeks at a time." Jerrod almost smiled. "We'd go hiking together. Just Dad and me."

"Sounds like you had fun."

"And we'd camp. We'd catch trout in the river and cook them over the campfire. Dad would teach me all about the stars and the constellations. He wanted to become an astrophysicist."

"Instead of taking over the family business?"

"It's what Mom wants me to do. I don't care about owning hotels. It's nice and all for people who want to do that, but I'd—" He stopped from saying what was on his mind and shook his head. "It doesn't matter. I have to get into Wheatly, graduate at the top of my class and get into Stanford. It's business school for me."

"You never know how things turn out. I went to Wheatly and loved it."

"Yeah, yeah." He nodded, holding up one hand. "I get it. I don't want to let anyone down, but I'd just like to do my thing, too."

"I found a way to make it work. My parents wanted me to study finance in college, and I did. I got a double major in education and finance. I found a way to do both. By that time I was on my own and the captain of my life."

"It sounds good. Anyway, I'm pretty much stuck here." He sighed. "You have a choice. You can leave."

"Are you kidding? I'm not going anywhere. I'm seeing this through with you."

"Do you think I can really pass the test?"

"Are you kidding? You'll ace it. Now, you'd better sneak back into the house before your mother sets the alarm system." Something crawled across her bare big toe. She flicked it off, refusing to consider what kind of bug or spider it was. "C'mon, kid."

"Okay." Jerrod followed her, dragging his feet.

"Think of it this way. It's another day down. There's only, what, fifteen to go?" She led the way across the grass. The grand house blazed in the night. "Once tomorrow is over, it will be fourteen."

"I get what you're saying. I'll hang in there. I won't have that test looming over my head forever." Jerrod tried another smile. The deck lights spilled over him as he trudged toward the house. "See ya tomorrow."

"See ya." She waited, watching until he was safely inside. *Just fifteen more days,* she told herself, and she was going back where she belonged—home.

Chapter Nine

❧

"I can handle the rest of this, birthday boy." Brandi grinned down at him from the tractor's air-conditioned cab. Christian music blared from the speakers, disrupting the serenity of the sun-swept fields. "Go on and gussy up. You've got to get ready for a party in your honor."

"Big deal. I turn thirty-one. I'm getting older, that's all it means." He did his best to show what he thought of that, but honestly, he liked any excuse for a get-together. He loved his family. He'd just wished Mom had called.

"You're over the hill, big brother," Brandi quipped sweetly. "Glad it's not me."

"Sure, but at least we get cake."

"Bree's bringing it from the bakery. Oops, that was supposed to be a surprise." She slapped both hands over her mouth.

"It's okay. I already guessed." He reached up to slide the compartment door closed. "See you in a bit and don't rock out too hard."

"Too late!" She turned up the volume and Christian music boomed, drowning out the crackle of mown grass beneath his boots as he trudged across the field. Nell jogged at his heels.

"Luke, hurry up!" Hunter's call echoed across the acres of cut grass drying in the blazing sun. "There's a call for you on the barn phone."

Probably business. He picked up his pace as Nell raced ahead, barking her pleasure at seeing Hunter in the barn's open doorway. Grazing cows in the nearby pasture lifted their heads to watch the goings-on curiously. Sweat beaded Luke's forehead and he swept off his hat, letting the hot puff of breeze dry him off.

He thanked his brother, clomped down the main barn's aisle and called out to the two late season calves awake in their pen. This time of day the barn was nearly empty with the doors thrown open and the milking parlor silent. His boots echoed in the rafters overhead as he stepped into the office.

"Hello?" He leaned the receiver against his shoulder so he had both hands free. "This is Luke."

"Hi, there." Mom's voice greeted him, thin with strain. "Happy birthday. Did you get my card?"

"The mail hasn't come yet today. Hi, Mom. How are you?" He dropped into the desk chair, plopped his hat down next to the computer and felt torn, as he always did. This was his mother, but he'd learned not to expect too much from her. That didn't stop him from wanting to be a good son. "How have you been?"

"Oh, you know. Trying to stay busy. I don't want to sit around too much and get fat."

It was hard to know what to say to that. "We'll miss seeing you today."

"It's too bad you couldn't come over here for your birthday."

"It's haying season. I have to be here. I'm sorry about that. We missed you at Brooke's wedding, too."

"It was arranged at the last minute, that's no way to get married, and it's such a long drive."

He could picture her in her house, soured on life, angry that her children had moved on without her. They'd had no choice. She'd stopped living long ago and opportunities had taken them far away from Miles City. He would always be thankful he and Hunter had landed a job at Wilson's Dairy, where they'd learned all they could about the business. It had made the difference in successfully running their dairy. He rubbed his forehead, wishing the relationship with his parents could be easier.

But you couldn't change other people. No matter how much you loved them. The only one you could change was yourself.

"You haven't seen hide nor hair of your father, have you?" Mom went on, and he answered patiently, listening to her troubles until Hunter knocked on the door. Luke felt empty as he said goodbye to her, even though he'd done all he could to repair that relationship.

He hauled out his cell phone, needing to hear Honor's voice, and decided against dialing her. That would make him feel better. Odd he hadn't heard from her today. He missed her. He hadn't mentioned his birthday to her, mostly out of shyness. It wasn't as if she could be here, anyway, since she had Jerrod to tutor. He wished he could see her.

That would be the best birthday present of all.

"Olive?" Honor peered around the archway leading into the family room. The spacious area felt cavernous, echoing the slightest sound. The space had been built for a family, but a lone figure sat in the corner, rigidly, so self-contained she could have turned to stone. "Are you okay?"

"I'll be fine." The woman's thick voice said otherwise. She gave a sniff. "How did Jerrod do on the practice test? His essay writing could see improvement."

"He's improved greatly. If he writes like this on his entrance exam, he'll be a shoo-in."

"That's a comfort. I want the best for him." Olive's chin went up as she squared her shoulders and launched off the sectional. Sunlight streamed over her, showing the trace of tears on her cheeks she'd clearly tried to swipe away. "How is his math coming along?"

"Better. I'm leaving him a set of problems to finish while I'm gone. That will keep him busy until suppertime."

"Fine. The exam is almost a week away."

"Thirteen days. And he'd doing fine." She could say that with confidence. "Just wanted you to know I'm on my way out."

"That's right. You're leaving early today."

"It's a friend's birthday."

"I didn't know you had any friends around here." Olive looked surprised and not exactly approving.

"I've made some good ones recently. A great blessing. I've got to get going if I'm going to make it on time. Have a good afternoon."

The instant she breezed out the door and into the blaze of the summer sun, her phone chimed with a text message. Eager to read what her friends were up to, she plucked it out of her bag and squinted at the screen.

R U on the way? Colbie wrote.

She juggled her keys, freeing up her thumbs to answer. Yes!

Awesome.

Another message arrived with a chime. This time from Bree. I've got the cake. YUM.

Don't nibble on it during the drive, Honor tapped in as she absently dropped behind her steering wheel.

Tempting! Bree answered. No guarantees.

Do U need directions? Colbie's message interrupted.

Already got 'em, she answered back. Thanks to the internet and an excellent map program. Thinking of the present she'd decided to buy, she typed. I'll see you at the bookstore first.

Meet ya there! Call if U get lost, Colbie responded. OK?

Promise. Honor hit send and another message popped on from Bree.

Can't wait. Ooh, this will B fun!

Totally, Honor sent back, tucked her phone in her bag and started the car. All she could think about was Luke. It was going to be so, so good to surprise him.

"Are you about ready?" Hunter knocked on the screen door frame.

"I'm just finishing up an email." Seated at his kitchen table, he frowned at his computer. Funny he hadn't heard from Honor yet today. That bummed him. He knew exactly why he couldn't stop missing her.

With his hair still a little damp from his shower, he reached down to pet Nell. Sleek and dark, she perked her ears and offered a toothy smile, his old friend. "Hey, good girl. Are you ready for a party?"

She rested her gray muzzle in his hands and let him

stroke her real good. He looked up when he heard the screen door hinges creak.

"You look way too happy." Hunter gazed in at him, frowning. "Guess you're still writing that California girl?"

"Considering your opinion on the matter, I'd rather not say." He grinned. He couldn't help it. He liked irritating his brother.

"Which means, yes. You know she's leaving soon, and she won't be coming back."

"How many times do you have to say it?" He gave Nell a final pat and shoved away from the table. "We're just friends."

"Tell that to someone who believes it." Hunter shook his head. "Women are trouble. That's why I'm smart enough to stay away from them."

"You mean they're smart enough to stay away from you," he quipped as he followed his brother out of the house.

"That may be." Hunter's boots hit grass, he patted a cow's rump as the animal looked up from grazing on the tasty dandelions. "Hey, there, Betty."

Betty mooed and swished her tail in answer.

"See? Some girls like me." Hunter winked.

"Dude, they're cows."

"Sure, but it's the principle. I'm not entirely unlikable."

"That's a matter of opinion." Actually, Hunter was a good guy, but he wasn't about to admit it.

Nell trotted along companionably, keeping one eye on the grazing cattle. Several cows glanced up to moo with interest when Luke unlatched the gate that blocked the driveway. Time to get them into a pasture before his sisters started driving up. He'd almost asked Honor

Send For
2 FREE BOOKS
Today!

I accept your offer!

Please send me two free
Love Inspired® novels and two
mystery gifts (gifts worth about
$10). I understand that these
books are completely free—
even the shipping and handling
will be paid—and I am under
no obligation to purchase
anything, ever, as explained on the
back of this card.

❏ I prefer the regular-print edition
105/305 IDL FS6A

❏ I prefer the larger-print edition
122/322 IDL FS6A

Please Print

FIRST NAME

LAST NAME

ADDRESS

APT.#   -   CITY

STATE/PROV.   ZIP/POSTAL CODE

Visit us online at
www.ReaderService.com

Offer limited to one per household and not applicable to series that subscriber is currently receiving.
Your Privacy—The Reader Service is committed to protecting your privacy. Our Privacy Policy is available
online at www.ReaderService.com or upon request from the Reader Service. We make a portion of our mailing
list available to reputable third parties that offer products we believe may interest you. If you prefer that we not
exchange your name with third parties, or if you wish to clarify or modify your communication preferences, please
visit us at www.ReaderService.com/consumerschoice or write to us at Reader Service Preference Service, P.O. Box
9062, Buffalo, NY 14269. Include your complete name and address.

if she could come, although he knew she was tied up with her tutoring job. In the end, he'd decided against it. It was best this way. No sense getting more attached. Days were ticking by fast and at this rate she would be gone in a blink.

The purr of an engine grabbed his attention. Tires crunched on the gravel on the sunny side of the barn as a luxury car idled in the driveway. The door swung open and a tall, willowy blonde climbed out. His jaw dropped. His pulse stalled.

"Hi, cowboy." She shaded her eyes with one slender hand. "Guess you're pretty surprised to see me."

"A little." Had he dreamed her up? He blinked a couple of times, but she was still there as real as could be. "What are you doing here? I mean, you came. I—"

"It's a surprise." Honor whipped on a floppy brimmed hat and a pair of round sunglasses. "It was Colbie's idea."

Colbie. He should have known.

"It looks like I've caught you at a bad time. You're busy." She tipped her head back to get a better view of him. Her long blond hair tumbled over her shoulder.

She was the prettiest sight. His throat ached just looking at her.

"Did you know there's a cow chewing on your shirt collar?" She tilted her head to one side, making her hat brim flap.

"That's Betty." He shrugged, dislodging the animal's grip. "She's friendly but too curious for her own good, and sometimes mine. Aren't ya, girl?"

The big white cow with big black spots pricked her bovine ears, studied Honor with curious brown eyes and stretched her neck across the gate with a friendly moo.

"Uh, hello, Betty," Honor greeted, amused.

"What do you think of your first cow encounter?"

"She's bigger than I expected and much more forth-right."

"She loves hats. My guess is she's taken a shine to yours. Out of the way, Miss Trouble." He shouldered the animal gently away from the gate. "Honor, sorry about this. Hunter and I were about to move the cows back into their pasture."

"I don't mind."

"Really? I thought you weren't an outdoors type."

"That doesn't mean I don't like animals. Hi, girl." She leaned over the gate to pet the friendly cow's nose.

Betty's chocolate-brown eyes softened with glints of adoration. She batted her long curly lashes.

"I like her. She's so sweet." Honor flashed a perfect smile his way.

It was hard not to adore her more. The delight on her face and the kindness of her touch. The effect on his heart was monumental. He'd never pictured her here, like this, taking delight in his simple farm life.

"Oh, and happy birthday to you. I'm a little early for the party, I think. Colbie had to swing home and pick up Lil, so I came out on my own."

"You didn't get lost?"

"I figured I might. That's why I allowed myself extra time fearing there might be some other road disaster. There wasn't, yay, and now I'm the first one here. I caught you in the middle of your work." She glanced up the hill where Hunter stood, frowning with impatience.

"No problem." Luke blinked, still not quite believing she was here. Talk about a welcome surprise. "We'll get Betty and her friends moved out and you can drive up to the house and park. It'll take a second."

"Okay." She gave Betty one final nose pet before

waltzing away from the gate. Elegant. That was the perfect word to describe her. Long and lean, standing against the background of wildflowers and meadow, in a tailored blouse and slim tan shorts. Her golden hair danced in the wind.

You're from two different worlds, he told himself, hiking up the driveway. It wasn't as if she belonged here. She wasn't going to stay.

"C'mon, Mildred and Louise." He whistled. "What do you girls think you're doing?"

Two sets of unrepentant brown eyes met his. With a tail swish, both old ladies backed down the steps and swung around to join him. The back of his neck tingled. Sure enough, Honor was watching him. She slid off her sunglasses, meeting his gaze.

You have to fight it, he told himself. *Keep control of your heart.*

That was going to be a losing battle. He gave Betty a pat on the shoulder as she ambled through the gate Hunter held open. A distant toot of a car horn told him the partygoers had arrived. Colbie's SUV turned off the county road and onto the driveway. Lil waved at him from the passenger seat as his sister hung out her open window, calling to Honor.

Honor. Sure, he was touched she'd come all this way for his birthday. Just remember not to read too much into it. This was just another social event. Just a way for her to spend time while she was here. No amount of his wishing would change that.

One thing for sure, the McKaslins knew how to laugh. Honor's sides hurt as she watched Luke carry the platter from the barbecue grill to the patio picnic table. His tall good looks, the strength of his silhouette against the stunning blue sky and the way his gaze found hers stole her breath.

She didn't want it to.

"He's such a sweetheart." Lil leaned in, eyes twinkling. "He comes all the way into town a few nights a month just to stay with me so Colbie can go out on the town."

"Go out on the town? Mother." Colbie rolled her eyes. "Usually it's Bible study. There's no handsome men to wink at."

"I'm just saying." Lil reached for her glass of lemonade. "Luke's a good man. They don't make many like him these days."

"Are you talking about me again?" Luke slid onto the end of the picnic table bench and set the platter on the table. Smoke rose from the charred burgers. "Lil has a terrible habit of telling lies about me."

"I do not tell lies!" Lil gasped. "I hardly even exaggerate."

"The problem is you, Luke." Honor grabbed a French fry and dragged it through a puddle of tartar sauce.

"Yes, it's totally Luke's fault," Brandi leaned in to grab the ketchup bottle.

"If he wasn't so wonderful—" Bree started to say.

"He's not that wonderful," Brooke interrupted with a mischievous grin. "You didn't grow up with him."

"The stories we could tell." Hunter took a hamburger patty off the platter. "That would change everybody's opinion of him real fast."

"We don't need to go digging up the past." Luke flushed, good-natured, cracking open a fresh hamburger bun. "I say, forgive and forget. Honor doesn't need to hear about my misspent youth."

"Sure I do. Think of all the emails he sent me." She

dragged another fry through the puddle of tartar. "How did I know he was telling the truth? He could have been fibbing. How did I know he was as good as he seemed?"

"That's what we're for." Colbie reached for the potato salad bowl and spooned a second helping onto her mom's plate. "We'll give you the low-down. We'll tell you what the real Luke McKaslin is like."

"No more just getting Luke's side of things," Bree chimed in.

"We'll tell it like it is," Brooke added.

"So prepare yourself." Brandi squeezed the ketchup bottle, aiming it over her pile of fries. "It's a sordid story."

"I'm prepared for the truth," Honor admitted, watching as Hunter offered the platter to Colbie, who shook her head no.

"First off, he would sneak through the house at Christmas time and find every present Mom had hidden away." Brooke glanced at her brother with a sister's gentle love.

"You didn't." Honor went for another fry. "I'm shocked."

"I can be shocking," Luke admitted.

"Then he would carefully peel off the tape, press back the paper to see what it was."

"Keep in mind, it wasn't necessarily his gift," Hunter chimed in and nudged the platter in Honor's direction.

She shook her head and gathered her half-eaten burger. Hunter held the platter to Luke.

"Hey, I was curious." Luke forked a patty onto his plate and reached for the mayo. "I was seven."

"He knew what we got before we did." Brooke smiled when her husband scooted closer on the bench and settled his arm around her shoulder. Happiness touched her like the golden sunlight. "He let us know it, too."

"He told you what you were getting? Before Christmas?" Honor pretended to be shocked.

"No, he teased us about it. 'I know what you're getting,' he used to say." Brooke snuggled against her husband. "Over and over again, like he knew this great big secret."

"Drove us nuts," Hunter added.

"Luke? Did you really used to do that, honey?" Lil, who looked a little pale, feigned disapproval. "I can't believe it. And here I assumed you'd been a sweet little boy."

"Me, too," Bree agreed, seated beside her fiancé, looking just as blissful as Brooke did. She shook her head, scattering her long blond hair over her shoulders. "I'm totally disappointed in you."

"Ditto." Brandi nodded, an exact duplicate of her twin. "So glad we didn't grow up in the same family."

"Exactly," Bree added, struggling not to laugh.

"I'm appalled," Colbie piped in, biting her lip to keep from laughing. "I'll never look at you the same way again."

"Justly deserved." Hunter took the mayo bottle from Luke and gave it a squeeze. "Right before we opened the presents, when we were sitting on the living room floor untying the bow—"

"Would he blurt it out?" Honor asked.

"Guilty." Dimples flashed as Luke bowed his head sheepishly. "I know, I know. I couldn't help myself. I was a kid."

"Still don't know why I put up with him," Hunter teased gruffly.

Hard to miss the brotherly affection. Harder to miss

the enduring ties that bound the family together as one, in spite of their different pasts and experiences. Love held that power.

"What can I say?" Luke shrugged. "I've reformed."

"Not entirely," Hunter argued. "I have one word for you. M&Ms."

"Fine, I have no self-control with those things. Do you have to bring that up? This is my birthday." Luke's laughter led the way. Honor found herself laughing, too, along with everyone else.

For this moment in time, this was exactly the place she wanted to be.

Chapter Ten

"Your family is so fun." Honor carried the stack of dessert plates to Luke's kitchen sink. "I can't remember the last time I laughed so much."

"They are easy on the funny bone, that's for sure." Towering over her, he took the dishes and lowered them into the sink.

"So are you."

"I'm glad you think I'm funny. Plenty of women don't."

"Wait. I meant funny-looking."

"Ha ha." He reached down to scratch Nell's ears, who had awoken at the sound of their voices. The old dog panted drowsily before slipping back to sleep on her bed in the corner. "It's time to feed the calves. Did you want to come? You could meet Faith."

"The calf I named? Count me in." She glanced at the luminous clock. She really should head back, it was a long drive. But how could she resist?

"Thanks again for the book." He opened the front door for her, where sunshine led the way onto a roomy covered porch.

"I knew just the one you wanted, since it's the next

book for discussion on Good Books." She liked the porch swing. Wouldn't that be a great place to stretch out and read in the evenings? "Next time maybe we can actually make it to the discussion instead of chatting at each other for two hours."

"Next time? No way. You'll be busy packing up to head home."

"I didn't bring much. Just what would fit in my car. So not a lot of packing time." She hopped down the porch steps. "Instead, I'll have lots of chatting with you time."

"Good to know. I'll take advantage of it while I can."

"What does that mean?"

"Once you get back to your life, you won't have as much free time. Admit it."

"I'm trying not to." She'd rather stay fixed in the here and now and not think about what lay ahead. She savored the warm puff of wind dancing through her hair and breathed in the crisp green scent of ripening wild grasses and freely blooming roses. They grew in a big clump, taking over the fence by the road, as if they'd been growing for decades. Wildflowers danced in the sun, nodding their faces and the grassy hillsides. Rolling fields, amber hills and craggy mountains rimming the horizon of the wide-open sky. Breathtaking. The kind of scenery that grew on you. "You have a beautiful place. And the view? Incredible. You must never get tired of it."

"True. It's one of the perks of my job."

"What a perk." Grass crunched beneath her sandals as they headed down the hill. "I'm an ocean girl. I love everything about it. The smell, the way it sweeps against the sand, the way it looks dark and roiling in a storm. But this is a close second. Hi, Betty."

The cow leaned against the fence, reaching out with her tongue.

"No, pretty girl, you can't have Honor's hat." Luke rubbed the outstretched nose as they ambled into the shade of a big white barn.

Sunlight tumbled through the open, wide doors, gilding the barn's main aisle with a fall of gold. Dust motes glittered in the air while stray bits of straw and hay fluttered in the hot summer breezes. Honor breathed in the pleasant scent of alfalfa, marveling how clean the concrete was beneath her sandals. Every surface she saw gleamed.

A small, baleful moo sounded from one of the roomy pens.

"That would be Barney." Luke led the way toward the nearest roomy enclosure. Straw rustled and a tiny moo bleated out. "There she is lying down. Guess we woke her up."

"She's the cutest thing I've ever seen." Her heart squeezed at the sight of the little black-and-white bundle curled up in soft straw. Faith lifted her little head, pricked her adorable ears and blinked her sleepy eyes. "Okay, now I'm wrapped around her hoof."

"I know the feeling."

Faith crawled onto her knees before scrambling awkwardly to a stand. Her knock-knees wobbled and she blinked big brown eyes. She ambled up to the rail and licked Honor's hand with a rough, pink tongue

"Hello, little one." She marveled at the darling personality reflected in those melted-chocolate eyes. The calf gazed up at Honor with a curious expression that could have meant, *are you my mama, too?*

Sweet. Her chest ached it felt so full. "This is how

you spend your days? Taking care of darling little things like Faith?"

"It's a tough job, but someone's got to do it."

Footsteps echoed in the aisle behind them. Hunter swang into sight carrying two large plastic bottles. Behind him she caught a glimpse of what must be the milking parlor, empty and sparkling clean.

"What do you mean? I feel like I do all the work around here." Hunter winked at her, his jet-black hair tumbling over his forehead. He thrust the bottles at Luke and winked. "Get busy and earn your way, slacker."

"Speak for yourself," he quipped, as Hunter headed back toward the milking parlor. Luke shook his head. "Would you like to help feed them?"

"Try and stop me." She accepted the bottle he handed her. The babies, spotting dinner, danced in place, crying with excitement. Warmth penetrated the plastic-like comfort as she watched Luke tuck the bottle in the crook of one arm. She did the same. Faith latched on with eager speed, emptying the bottle at a fast rate and swinging her tail with contentment. Nothing could be cuter than the little creature with her big baby eyes searching hers with loving adoration.

Thump went her heart. *For the calf,* she told herself. Not for the man beside her.

That was when she finally noticed the soft notes lulling from overhead speakers. "Is that Beethoven?"

"One of his piano concertos, sounds like." Luke nodded. "The cows also like audiobooks, but it depends on the book."

"Too bad they can't post reviews on Good Books."

"It's hard to type when you've got hooves."

She shook her head at him. "Bad. Totally bad."

His violet eyes twinkled back at her. Barney chose

that moment to head-butt his bottle; it flew out of the crook of Luke's arm and skidded across the aisle, empty. "Oops. Hold on to yours tight—"

Wham! The bottle jumped out of her hands and clattered on the concrete. She laughed, she couldn't help it.

"We're one stooge short," Luke quipped as he grabbed her bottle, too.

She had a soft spot for a man who could make her laugh. She hated that the feeding was over, that she had no excuse to stay a moment longer and spend time with the man she liked so well.

Caring like this wasn't what she'd signed up for. Affection warmed her heart against her will. She didn't want to feel this way. Not so soon after ending another relationship. She simply wasn't ready.

"Luke!" Hunter's boots hammered in the aisle, the alarm in his stride shattering the merriment.

"What's wrong?" Luke straightened up, instantly solemn.

"We've got to get up to the house. There's a problem with Lil."

"Is she okay?"

"She's not feeling well." Worry slashed across Hunter's face as he slid his cell into his pocket. "It's serious. Colbie's called an ambulance."

"What?" Stricken, Luke shoved the empty bottles onto the top of a grain barrel lid. "No, this isn't some kind of a joke, is it?"

"You know I wouldn't joke about this." Strain snapped along Hunter's jaw. "Go on, get up to the house and be with her. I'll stay here and finish feeding."

"Then you'll be up?"

"Count on it. I'll do what needs to be done." Grim, Hunter grabbed a pitchfork. "Go on, you two. Colbie may need help."

"We're on it." He hated leaving his brother behind. He reached for Honor's hand, grateful for the warmth of her fingers against his. A comfort he hadn't even known he needed. Lil was like a mom to him.

"An ambulance? That worries me. Colbie isn't one to overreact. Let Lil be okay." The words were more prayer than a wish as he hurried outside.

"I'm praying as hard as I can," Honor told him.

They weren't halfway to the house when tires crunched on the gravel driveway behind them. The ambulance barreled up the lane and he stepped aside, standing with Honor as the vehicle hurried by. Poor Lil. This was serious, whatever had happened. Colbie dashed into sight on the front lawn, waving to the driver. Her look of desperation made his eyes burn.

He didn't remember dashing up the hill or crossing the lawn, all he knew was the kick of fear seeing the medics surrounding Lil. She lay on a gurney, trying to answer questions in a slurring voice. He spotted Colbie hovering over her mom, carefully watching the medics, reciting the list of medications Lil used to help control her MS symptoms.

"She looks so tiny lying here." He hated being helpless. That slurred speech troubled him. Was she going to be okay? He needed to do something. Save her. Fix her. Help her. Just something. He felt useless standing there.

"God is with her no matter what." Honor squeezed his hand, holding on, offering him comfort.

That about broke him. He gritted his teeth, determined not to lean on her. Knowing she was offering him her friendship, not her heart.

That was a great comfort. *Father, please watch over Lil. We can't lose her.*

"They're taking her to Bozeman." Brooke hurried

over, tears damp on her face. "Liam's driving Colbie's car, so she can ride in the ambulance with her mom."

"Mac's called ahead. He knows a lot of the hospital staff." Bree scampered over. "Brandi and I are going to lock up here, so you can go to Bozeman."

Honor's hand tightened around his, holding on, re-assuring him, letting him know she was there for him.

It wasn't smart, but his fingers tightened around hers right back, needing her more than was wise to admit.

"You can go home, you know." Luke leaned closer in his waiting room chair, his voice rumbling low against Honor's ear. "It might be a long wait, and you have a long drive ahead of you. You might want to get home before dark falls."

"True." It didn't feel right to up and leave the worried family behind, these people she cared about. "I'm staying. I'm a little sweet on Lil. I want to make sure she's okay."

"Me, too. Waiting is the worst. Not knowing."

"Fearing things are worse than they are."

"It's killing me." Luke's face twisted with agony. "There's Hunter."

Sure enough, the tall, dark-haired man strode through the automated doors and into the crowded waiting room. His gaze locked on Luke's, their brotherly bond obvious. Luke stood, released her hand and met Hunter halfway across the crowded room. Their heads bent together as they spoke. Impossible to hear what they said.

"I just wish there was something we could do," Brooke spoke up, seated on Honor's other side. "I feel so useless."

"So do I." She thought of the gentle, sweet woman being wheeled into the ambulance. A reminder that just like that, life could change. You never knew what might lie ahead. The future was always a mystery. Only God knew. "I wonder how Colbie is doing."

"She's got to be falling apart on the inside, although she'd never show it. She's a rock in a crisis." Brooke's voice armed with affection for her sister.

"She takes amazing care of Lil," Bree leaned across the aisle to chime in. "I don't know how she does it."

"She blows me away," Brandi agreed. "Everything she does for her mom? Her whole life is devoted to Lil."

"It's why she doesn't date," Brooke sympathized. "She has no time and big responsibilities."

Honor felt a tingle against her cheek, looked up and the din of the waiting room silenced. Luke's gaze met hers and she could read his look like a book. Unaware of getting out of her chair, she found herself walking toward him, laying her hand against his outstretched palm and understanding what he needed most. So, she held on tight.

"Colbie!" Brooke called out. "How is she?"

The rest of the McKaslins flocked toward the tall, slim woman standing by the admitting desk. Tears had dried on Colbie's cheeks. "Mom's done with her CT scan and they are giving her an IV. It's supposed to break up the clot in her brain. We're praying it works."

"It will. Positive thinking, positive praying." Brandi wrapped her arms around Colbie.

"That's right. We'll pray as hard as we can." Brooke joined the pair, hugging them both.

"Good, because I'm not ready to lose her." Colbie blinked away tears, leaning on her sisters as Bree moved in, completing the circle of sisters, clinging to one another. "Mom will just have to get better and that medicine will just have to work. I'm not accepting any other outcome."

"Neither am I," Honor added. Brandi drew her in and she joined the hug. She clung to them, remembering how frail Lil had looked before they'd closed the ambulance doors. Lil, who had a smile and a kind word for everyone and her indomitable cheer. Honor blinked, surprised to find tears in her eyes, too.

"Hang in there, Colbie." Hunter's gruff baritone grated with emotion. "She'll be okay."

"She better be." Luke swallowed hard and squared his shoulders. "She's the best Friday night date I've ever had."

"Mom is sweet on you." Colbie smiled through her tears.

"Tell her I expect to spend more Friday nights with her watching *Jeopardy!* She beats me every time." He cleared his throat, leaving so much unspoken, like always. He loved Lil. She was the mom he didn't have. "Tell her I intend to win next time. My ego is on the line."

"I'll tell her." Tears tracked down Colbie's cheeks. She understood the words he couldn't say.

Honor did, too. Her touch on his arm made his throat ache. He held in a lot of truth about his feelings for her. Not sure what he could do about that, but now wasn't the time or place to worry about it.

"I'd better get back to her." Colbie swiped at her tears. "Thanks, guys, for being here."

"Where else would we be?" Hunter asked, giving her a hug.

"We're here for as long as it takes." Luke thought of the cows at home and the responsibilities there. He and Hunter would take turns going back to the ranch at milking and feeding times, and there was always Milton, the foreman of the neighboring ranch who would pitch in. They could make it work.

"We're going on a cafeteria run." Brandi rubbed the last of her tears from her eyes. "Tea all around?"

"Make mine coffee," Hunter said, reaching into his back pocket.

"I got it." Luke beat him to the punch, handing over a twenty. "Tea for me. Honor?"

"Peppermint." She blinked her damp lashes. He liked her more for that. That she was here, when she could have left. That she cared. She stayed at his side, and when he slipped an arm around her shoulder, she moved in, snuggling against him, stealing his heart a little more.

"Mom's settled in her room." In the waiting room, Colbie hugged her sisters one by one. "She's resting comfortably. I wish visiting hours weren't over, but you can see her in the morning. Honor, why are you still here?"

"Where else would I be?" She hugged Colbie, too. The poor woman looked exhausted with stress and worry. It was clear how much she loved her mother.

"You're a keeper. I'm so glad we're friends." Colbie gave her an extra squeeze. "Thank you."

Honor stepped back so the twins could move in and hug their sister good-night. Her family wasn't a touchy-feely kind. When her dad had been rushed to the hospital for a minor heart attack three years ago, everyone had waited stoically and pragmatically. Tears were held back in her family.

So was affection. Feelings were held in at all costs. She rather liked the way the McKaslins did it. Tears and hugs and messages of love were relayed to Colbie to be given to Lil when she woke up. Promises to call if Colbie needed anything—anything—and Luke moseying up to make sure there wasn't more he could do.

"Mac and I will drop by and pick up a change of clothes for you," Bree offered, reaching for her tall, strapping fiancé's hand. "We'll close the curtains and bring in the mail."

"I'll come by early and bring you breakfast," Brooke offered.

After their goodbyes, the family broke apart. Colbie hurried to her mother's bedside. Honor joined the rest of the family heading toward the exit. In silence from exhaustion and worry, they pushed through the doors and spilled into the warm summer night.

"I can't believe it's after midnight." Luke's baritone rumbled near her ear. "Are you going to be okay driving back?"

"Sure. I'll be fine." Except for the yawn she had to stifle. Oops. Exhaustion weighed on her. "I'll find a drive-thru and order a cup of strong coffee. That's all I need."

"Or you could come home with us," Brandi offered.

"She can have my bed," Bree offered. "I'll take the couch."

"No way am I kicking you out of your bed." She knew the twins shared an apartment. "I'll take the couch."

"Forget it. You're a guest," Bree said sweetly as she headed in the direction of Mac's gleaming pickup. "We'll make it work."

"Thanks, guys." A good solution. It was better not to drive when she was this tired, and she'd be here tomorrow to help out as much as she could. Since it was Sunday, she would have the whole day free to lend a hand.

"Guess I'll see you tomorrow." Luke walked her to her car, parked next to his truck.

"Guess so."

He brushed a strand of hair out of her eyes. A dangerous move and she knew it, but did she stop him? No way. Not even a little bit. At the gentle sweep of his fingertips against her forehead and the caring dark in his eyes, what did her feelings do? They tumbled long and slow.

Okay, *maybe* it was time to admit this might be more than a little crush, but nothing to worry about, right? At least that was what she hoped as Luke opened her door for her. She was *so* not ready to feel this way. "Good night, Luke."

"'Night." He closed her door as soon as she was settled behind the wheel. She watched him circle toward his truck, his silhouette striking against the background of a velvet black sky and twinkling stars.

If only he didn't take a piece of her heart with him.

Chapter Eleven

It had been hard to leave the hospital that morning, and the weight of it felt heavy on Luke's heart as he climbed the church steps. The early service was over, the doors flung wide and worshippers began streaming out. Lots of folks stopped him to ask about Lil, and it was a comfort to know so many of their church family were praying for her swift recovery.

She'd been still and pale when he'd left her side. He'd come early to do what he could for her, to sit with Lil so Colbie could shower and change. Lil wasn't able to speak and it broke his heart. Bleary-eyed, he struggled down the aisle against the current, searching for the one face he longed to see.

There she was, seated alongside his sisters with her head bowed in prayer, oblivious to the clamor and clatter surrounding her. The soft jeweled light from the stained glass windows tumbled over her, and the sight brought peace to his heart. Honor did that to him.

He waited until her prayer ended and she lifted her head. He knelt in the aisle so he was eye level with her. "Hey there, stranger."

"You missed the service."

"The early service," he corrected. "I took the first shift at the hospital so Colbie could…"

"…catch the service, I know." Honor nodded to Colbie, who sat next to her, still praying hard. "Is Hunter with Lil?"

"He shooed me out. Wouldn't take no for an answer." What he could say was how hard it had been. He'd barely slept last night, fearing the phone would ring with even worse news. Hunter, bless him, had stayed behind to sit with Lil.

"My big brothers are the best." Colbie lifted her head, her prayer done. Tears stood in her eyes. "How was Mom looking?"

"Okay." He couldn't make himself say how pale she'd been and how groggy and confused when the nurses had come in to tend her.

"I've got to go." Colbie bopped to her feet.

"Of course you do." Honor stood to move out of her way. "Give Lil a hug from me."

"You know I will. Thanks." Colbie blinked back tears, too tough to let them fall.

"Have you eaten?" he asked, remembering how she'd refused the breakfast Brooke had brought her. Too upset to eat, she'd said. "Maybe we can get you—"

"No. What if Mom needs me? I've got to be there for her." Colbie shook her head, shouldering into the aisle. "I'll eat something at the hospital later."

"Promise, or I'll hunt you down." He winked.

"Sure, sure." She took a step, not watching where she was going and smashed straight into someone in the aisle. Her Bible went flying.

"Excuse me," said a deep voice. "Are you all right?"

"Oh, I'm so sorry. I wasn't watching where I was—"

Colbie stopped, obviously startled. "—going. Aren't you the district—"

"—attorney," Bree finished, bopping into the aisle. "Hi, Austin. Did you enjoy the service?"

"I did." The tall man knelt to fetch Colbie's Bible. "It's good to see the McKaslin family again."

"Austin's been looking for a new church," Bree explained. She'd gotten to know the district attorney and his staff when she'd been a primary witness on a murder trial a few months back. "I thought he might like it here."

"I do." His granite face softened with kindness when he looked at Colbie. He handed her the Bible. "I heard about your mother. Will she be all right?"

"Absolutely. Mom will pull out of this just fine." Her chin lifted, as if she refused to consider any other outcome. "Thanks."

"I'll keep her in my prayers."

"That's nice of you." She blushed, not making eye contact. "It was good seeing you again. As for the rest of you, I'll catch you all later."

"Count on it." Luke noticed the district attorney watched Colbie as she dashed down the crowded aisle, quickly disappearing from sight.

Interesting. But chances were one hundred percent that Austin Quinn would never do more than look. Not many men would want to take on a woman who had the sole responsibility for her ill mother.

Austin left with a nod of farewell.

"Okay, everyone has their to-do lists?" Brooke asked as she tumbled into the aisle.

"Yes." Bree held up a small sheet of paper.

"Me, too!" Brandi held up hers.

"Then let's get at it." Brooke speared him with a look. "You'll pick up lunch for everyone, right?"

"I printed off the email you sent early this morning." He patted his shirt pocket. "I've got my assignments and fully intend to execute them."

"Hey, what about me? I didn't get a list." Honor looked unhappy about that. "My computer is in my room above the Lamberts' garage, so I could have gotten one, but how would I know, as I didn't go home last night?"

"Well, that explanation is simple. You don't have a list because I didn't make one for you," Brooke offered gently. "You're a guest, remember?"

"I was hoping I was a friend."

Why a lump lodged in his throat, he couldn't say. He didn't want to be touched by Honor's caring. She liked his family. He knew she did. But her giving up her day off to help his family, that got to him.

Big time.

"You're a *good* friend," Broke corrected, her eyes swimming with gratitude. "Okay, you talked me into it. I'll give you a few things off my list. How's that?"

"Perfect." She waited for Brooke to tear off the bottom items from her list and accepted the scrap gladly. "You have my cell. If you need anything else, just call."

"Will do." Brooke headed backwards down the aisle. "See you back at the hospital around noonish."

"Whatever you do, don't forget lunch, Luke," Brandi called out.

"Yeah, cuz we'll be hungry," Bree gave a finger wave as she disappeared out the door.

The new wave of worshippers for the second service began to trickle in. There was no time or privacy to say the things on his mind, so he gave Honor his best attempt at a smile. "Let's see what Brooke gave you."

"I have no gardening skills whatsoever." She held up her list. "Do you think I can keep Lil's roses alive for one day?"

"I have faith in you." He skimmed the few items in Brooke's tidy script. "The house key is in a ceramic ladybug in the flower bed next to the front steps. You can't miss it. Madge from next door might come over to see what you're up to. She's a nice lady."

"Good. Maybe she can offer advice on my watering skills." She tucked the list in the pocket of what looked like a dress borrowed from the twins. "Guess I'll see you at the hospital."

"I'll be the one with the sandwiches."

"What about those little bags of chips?" She backed down the aisle, into the fall of the stained glass sunlight.

"Do you like baked or regular chips?"

"Barbecue." She shook her head. "You have a lot to learn about me, Luke McKaslin."

"Most of our interactions have been on the computer, where I haven't witnessed your chip-eating preferences."

"I sort of like this real-time thing we're doing."

"So do I."

"I'm sorry about the circumstances, but I'm glad I'm here." The words popped out, unedited and honest, weighing with more meaning than she'd intended. What would Luke think if he knew her feelings toward him were changing?

"It's not a hardship having you around." The tone in his voice and the warmth in his eyes *could* be saying more than friendship.

Wasn't that a scary thought? But likely it was only her imagination, she decided, as Luke held up a hand in farewell.

"Call if you have any problems," he invited, standing strong and solid. Her pulse skipped three beats.

"Right." Rattled, she banged her shoulder against the door frame, bounced off it and tripped on the top step. Good thing there was a railing for her to grab or she would have tumbled all the way down. For a moment, she'd almost let herself believe Luke's feelings changing for her, too.

She joined the mob in the parking lot. Kids shouted, conversations rang and engines rolled over as she crossed the blazing hot pavement. A beep, beep of a horn caught her attention. Bree's little white pickup zipped by, two rows over. Both twins waved at her.

She waved back.

Now, where had she parked? She couldn't see her car anywhere. Why? Because her brains had suddenly scrambled. What could the only rational reason be for that?

Because I'm falling for him, that's why. Which was totally crazy. Completely inconvenient. She stumbled to the first row of cars, oblivious to the comings and goings around her. She didn't want to be vulnerable. Not again. That was like walking through a mine field waiting for an explosive device to go off and take your heart with it.

Her cell rang. She scooped it out of her handbag and didn't look at the screen. The instant she heard his voice, calm spread through her. The sun brightened.

"Hey, I forgot to ask what kind of sandwich you like." His voice had to be her new most favorite sound.

"Turkey is fine." She felt a tingle on the back of her neck and spun around.

"Turkey it is. Mayo? You like mustard, right?"

"Right."

On the top church step, the sunlight found him, bronzing him with light. As if saying, here, what about this one?

I'm not looking, she wanted to say. *Remember Kip? Love and romance are such a bad idea.*

"Okay, I wanted to make sure. Besides, it gave me a reason to call." His smile held enough magnetism to hold her, even across the length of the parking lot. She felt trapped like the moon to the earth, unable to move away as the wind ruffled his sandy hair.

No one had ever been so dear to her.

The blast of a car horn rocked her out of her thoughts. She blinked, realizing she stood in front of a minivan waiting to pull out.

"Sorry." She hopped out of the way, listening to the rumble of Luke's chuckle in her ear.

"It's crazy out there. I should let you go."

"Yes, before I create a traffic jam," she agreed, as two vehicles attempted to scoot into the spot vacated by the minivan. She was definitely in the way again as a station wagon idled, waiting for her to cross in front of it. "If I can just find my—"

"—car?" He finished. "I see it. One row over. Two cars toward the church."

"Thanks." Had she gone blind? She cut between parked cars, stuffing her phone into her bag. Love messed with your common sense. It ruined your judgment. It was a land mine waiting to go off. But did that stop her heart?

No way. She glanced over her shoulder just in time

to see Luke striding back inside the church. She gave a little sigh as she leaned against her car.

And if she had to fall, why did it have to be for a Montana cowboy?

"Why?" She tilted her head back to ask God. The blue sky didn't answer, so she opened her door and dropped behind the wheel. This was not going according to her plan. She jammed her key into the ignition, forced her mind to the matter at hand and realized she didn't have directions to Colbie's place.

Wasn't it just too bad she'd have to call Luke one more time?

"Well, as long as Colbie says it's all right." The neighbor, Madge, adjusted her gardening gloves. "We keep a pretty close eye on what goes on around here. Keeps troublemakers away."

"I don't intend to make trouble." Honor unwound the hose across the front lawn. "Although I can't guarantee there won't be any."

"Do you know what you're doing, missy?" The older lady picked up her clippers. "You're going to ruin those shoes."

"They are the only ones I have." She'd left the borrowed heels and dress folded neatly inside Colbie's home, where she'd changed into shorts and a summery top. "I could go barefoot."

"I recommend it." Madge turned her attention to pruning her flowers, but she kept an obvious eye on the proceedings next door.

Okay, she was new to yard work, having nothing more than two flower pots on her apartment balcony to worry about, which were Kelsey's, but that didn't mean she couldn't figure this out. How hard could it be? She slipped off her shoes, tossed them onto the porch and plunked the sprinkler in the middle of the grass. Her cell chimed.

Missing U! Kelsey's text flashed on the screen. We're brunching after church. Guess where?

Surfs? Her favorite waterside restaurant. It was easy to picture the whole gang seated around a table.

It's not the same without U. Kelsey answered. Can't wait until U come home. Just wait 'til U hear.

There's news, Anna Louise's text popped up to say. Big-time, won't believe it news.

Tell me. Squinting in the direct sun, Honor hit send and squished across the spongy lawn, the blades of grass tickling the bottoms of her feet. What were the chances California schools were suddenly doing massive rehiring?

I'm ENGAGED.

Engaged? Honor dropped her phone. It plummeted into a rhododendron bush and disappeared. She felt a little dizzy when she dove in after it. With trembling hands, she typed, hardly able to contain her happiness. When? Why? Who?

Yesterday. I love him. Tom Jenkins, Anna Louise answered.

Why did that name sound familiar? She flicked a smudge of dirt off the screen as she thought about it. Is that the piano guy who came to tune the school pianos?

Yes! He fixed Mom's piano last month, I dropped by while he was there and the rest is history.

Definitely unbelievable. And fast! But when true love hit, what was a girl to do? She changed her life for it, that's what.

Awesome, she typed back. Ginormous congrats.

Thanx!

Honor leaned in beside the rhododendron bush, turned on the faucet and waited for the sprinkler to sprinkle.

It didn't. It sat there motionless. Not one drop of water shot into the air.

Okay, that was a small hiccup. Something was clearly wrong, but she could figure it out. She checked the hose connection, fine. She trailed it through the flower bed. Fine. She eyed the length of it across the front lawn. There was the problem. A kink in the hose.

So we've got a wedding to plan, Kelsey's text arrived next. We're gonna be bridesmaids!

Is that wise? Honor texted back with a smile. She stalked across the grass and gave the hose a tug.

Nothing. The kink remained.

Probably not, Anna Louise commented. It's a risk I'm willing to take. When U come home, we'll start planning.

Can't wait. She hit Send, picturing the fun her friends were having chatting away and sending texts while talking to one another. Yes, it would be great to be with them again. To hang with some of the people who mattered most.

So why did heaviness wrap around her like a damp blanket? Could it be she wasn't as excited about heading home as she'd once been?

Warning. There's gonna B lotsa shopping, Kelsey texted back. Can't wait. Miss U.

Miss U 2. Congrats again, Anna Louise. She tucked her phone in her back pocket so both hands would be free, hunkered over the kink in the hose and gave it a good twist. Twelve more days. Tomorrow would be eleven.

Cold water shot out of the sprinkler and pummeled her like torrential rain. It sluiced down her face, blinding her. It soaked her hair, it soaked her shirt. With a gasp, she leaped out of the stream only to have the sprinkler revolve and slam into her again.

"Bravo." Applause rang out as she finally jumped clear and rubbed water out of her eyes.

"I had counted on it shooting in the other direction." Dripping water, she tracked across the lawn on the safe side of the sprinkler. "What are you doing here?"

"I thought I'd swing by on my way to the sandwich shop to check on you. Make sure you weren't running into any problems. I'm too late."

"Why would you say that? There are no problems here." She shook her head like a dog. Water droplets scattered. "I've checked on the house, watered the houseplants, picked up the paper, watered all the beds. Just the lawns left to do."

"Maybe I'd better take over."

"I've got it. Go fetch your sandwiches."

"I'm going to lend a hand. End of story." Luke tucked his keys into his pocket, rocked off his truck's fender he'd been leaning against and stalked toward her. His shadow fell across her as big and bold as the man, and her breath caught sideways in her chest. A touch of panic and wishing melded together, freezing her in place—even as she heard the tick of the revolving sprinkler head and the patter of approaching water.

"C'mon here." His hand roped her wrist, tugged her out of the way at the last second and into the sanctuary of his strong arms. She breathed in the faint scent of fabric softener as her cheek came to rest against his cotton shirt. He was iron-strong man and cozy comfort.

Wow. The earth stopped spinning. Time ceased moving and in that frozen moment between one breath and the next, between one heartbeat and the next, she felt her world shift inexorably. Irrevocably. This was one place she wanted to stay forever, safe in the circle of his arms.

"That was a close one." As if he wasn't affected, not even the slightest bit, Luke stepped back, breaking the contact, putting distance between them. His easygoing grin, framed by dimples, didn't hold a trace of the amazement filling her.

"I can't believe you aren't thanking me. Your back could be as wet as your front." He winked, casual, friendly, everything she used to want him to be. That is, when she'd been lonely in her room above the Lamberts' garage missing home so much it hurt, his friendship had been the balm she'd needed.

Now it was far short of what she hoped for, far short of what she felt.

"Oh, I wasn't thinking. I got you wet." She winced at his damp silk tie and his dress shirt sporting wet splotches, thanks to her.

"No problem. I'll dry. You, on the other hand, are going to have to stand in the sun for a bit."

"I know. Look at me." Sagging hair, drooping clothes and water dripping from her chin. "I'm a total mess."

"No argument here." His fingertips grazed her cheek as he swept a shank of hair from her face. His gaze turned luminous and soft as if with affection, but it was hard to tell with the sun blazing in her eyes. When she blinked, the look was gone.

Just wishful thinking. Again.

"Luke?" A voice called from the neighbor's flower bed. "How is Lil doing this morning?"

"Improved." He turned away, the closeness between them gone.

Wait, correct that. Their *imagined* closeness.

"The doctors are cautiously optimistic." Luke ambled through the gravel toward the older lady. "The drug they gave her seemed to do its job."

"That's a big relief. Lil has enough challenges without adding more." Madge straightened from her clipping and pressed both hands to the small of her back. "I'm not as young as I used to be, that's a fact. Anyway, do they know how serious the stroke is?"

"She has limitations, but they are still assessing." A muscle twitched in his jaw. "She'll get through it. We're all behind her."

"That makes the difference." Madge nodded approvingly. "Is there anything I can do to help out?"

"There is." The wind tousled his thick hair, giving him a rakish touch. A nice contrast to his church clothes and tie. "We're about to go fetch lunch for everyone. Could you turn off the water in about twenty minutes?"

"Sure thing. I can take over watering this evening, too."

"Madge, you're a sweetheart."

"Don't I know it." The older lady winked.

"Then I guess we can get going." Luke held out his hand to Honor, palm up, dimples friendly. "Want to come with me? I could use help ordering all those sandwiches."

"And chips. Don't forget the chips." She kept it light, making him smile, to hide what burned in her heart. "Let me rescue my shoes. Oh! And my handbag and keys."

"Did you leave them inside?"

"You know I did." She timed her sprint across the wet grass with the arc of squirting water. When she reached the front steps, she couldn't resist the urge to glance over her shoulder. She drank in the sight of him standing on the other side of the spraying sprinkler, where sunlight made rainbows off the water droplets.

Just wishing, she told herself as she bent to grab her shoes. Never had she wanted anything as much as she wanted Luke's heart.

Chapter Twelve

"Are you meeting up with her today?" Hunter tossed up a bale of hay.

No need to ask who he meant by *her*. Luke grabbed the bale and hiked across the stacked hay beneath his boots. "That's the plan. I haven't heard from her yet."

"Maybe that's for the best."

"What does that mean? You don't like her?" Luke hefted the bale into place, swiped sweat off his forehead with the back of his leather gloves. It had been a tough few days juggling the haying needing to be done on top of being in Bozeman as much as they could to be with Lil. Honor's emails and phone calls checking up on him had been a great comfort.

One he didn't want to mention to his brother.

"What's not to like?" Hunter threw up another bale. "Honor is pretty and nice. The way she helped out on Sunday. Hard not to appreciate that."

"Sure it is." He did his best to hide his true feelings as he manhandled the bale into place. Good thing his back was turned so Hunter couldn't read his reaction. No doubt his hidden strengthened affection for Honor wasn't so hard to spot. Not if you knew how to look.

"She fits right in with our sisters, doesn't she? It's like they've always been friends."

"Hmm." Hunter appeared to think about that as he stalked across the nearly empty trailer and grabbed the last remaining hay bales. "You know what I've been thinking?"

"Not particularly."

"She does fit in pretty good for a city girl. A California girl." Hunter's glare became pointed.

"What are you trying to say?" Luke braced for it as he hiked the heavy bale into place.

"I overheard the girls talking about that purse she had on Sunday. It cost more than both our monthly truck payments combined."

"So?"

"I'm saying she wouldn't be happy fitting into this kind of life. That's all."

"You don't know that." Hard to keep the emotions from showing through, but he tried to laugh it off. Likely as not, he failed, but at least he tried. "Besides, I never figured she would want to fit in here. There's never been a chance for that."

"Sure. The head can know one thing, but the heart doesn't always listen. I've seen the way you look at her."

"There goes your overactive imagination again." Luke winked. It was impossible not to kid his brother.

"I'm just sayin'." Hunter shrugged, maybe seeing the truth, after all. "I don't want you to get hurt. One woman's already done that to you. Maybe you shouldn't go tonight."

"To the fundraiser for Lil's medical expenses?" Luke popped open a water bottle. "No way. I'm going. End of story."

"Then at least text that woman and tell her not to come."

"That's terrible advice."

"It's smart advice. I feel obligated to offer it. You've clearly lost all judgment when it comes to her."

"Oh, I've still got my judgment." It was his heart that he'd lost. As long as Honor didn't know it, then maybe it wouldn't hurt as bad when she left in eight days and counting.

The toot of a horn drew his attention. Brandi coming in behind the wheel of the tractor, hauling another ton of hay. His pocket buzzed. He hauled out his phone and checked the screen.

Leaving rite now, Honor wrote. C U soon.

Can't wait, he wanted to write. *It's all I'm thinking about,* he wanted to say. But when he hit Send, his message read, Great. Should B fun.

"Go on, both of you." Hunter hopped from the trailer and landed with a two-footed thud on the concrete. "I'll get this stacked. Go wash cars for Lil."

"You mean it?" Brandi flew from the tractor, her pigtails flying. "Awesome. You're fantastic. But what about all the milking and barn work? That's more than a one-man job."

"I can handle it. Do I look like I can't?"

"Ooh, I adore ya." Brandi gave Hunter a sisterly hug, ignoring his grumbles of protest. "Sorry, but you can't fool me."

"Not trying to." Hunter growled. "Now, get out of here."

"You're a softy beneath all that gruff." Brandi shaded her eyes with one hand, squinting into the sun. "Hey, Luke? Are you coming?"

"Couldn't keep me away with a stick," he quipped,

tucking his phone into his pocket. Sweat sluiced down the back of his neck as he hopped down from the growing mountain of hay, landing beside his brother. The roof of the pole building blocked his view of the sky, but the gathering thunderheads were hard to miss.

"That's the last of the cut," Hunter echoed what Luke was thinking. "Just in the nick of time. Don't worry, I'll get it under cover if rain hits. I just hope it holds off until after Lil's fundraiser."

"Me, too. Maybe it won't rain that far south." Thoughts of Honor stayed with him as he followed Brandi up the driveway. Betty leaned over the fence to moo at them. Brandi picked a handful of daisies and he couldn't stop grinning. He was going to see Honor again.

He couldn't wait.

She locked her car, tied her hair into a ponytail and slid on her sunglasses. Her pulse tripped with excitement as she crossed the church's parking lot. But not excitement at seeing Luke again, oh, no. As long as she didn't admit her deepened feelings, then she could pretend to be a breezy, in control woman who wasn't falling for the wrong man.

"Honor!" Bree's hand shot up. "Over here!"

"We're painting signs." Colbie jogged to catch up with her with a sack clutched in one arm. She'd obviously just arrived, too. "I can't believe you came. You're a true friend, Honor."

"Just returning the favor." She couldn't begin to say what the McKaslin sisters' friendship had meant to her. She'd been lonely for many long months during her stint in Montana. Not anymore. She had more texts, emails and calls than she knew what to do with. It was nice.

She nodded toward the group of people unwinding hoses and lining up buckets. "It looks like a lot of people have turned up to help."

"The entire volleyball team." Colbie set the bag down next to Bree. "And the opposing team. I couldn't believe it when their captain came up with the idea of a car wash. It just makes you think, you know?"

"That there's more good in the world than we realize?" Honor nodded. She believed that.

"It's nice to know when bad things happen, you're not alone." Brooke peered into the bag and took out a can of paint. "All right, who is the most artistic of us?"

"Bree," Brandi said.

"Brandi," Bree said.

"I possess modest sign-painting skills." Honor chose a brush from the sack.

"I knew I invited you for a reason." Colbie knelt on the blacktop, paint can in hand. "These are great. Who made the *A* boards? Wait. I don't need to ask. Luke and Hunter."

"Yes. All they need is signage." Brandi handed over a paintbrush. "Which means we can go help with something else."

"Totally."

"Oh, go on with you." Colbie pointed with her paintbrush, amused. "Make yourself useful somewhere else. We won't miss you."

"Sure you will. Wait, they're setting up the money taker's table. That would be me." Brandi bopped away with her twin.

"And me," Bree chimed in.

"Those two. Nothing but trouble." Brooke smirked, studying Honor's lettering work with great consideration as her apparent role as supervisor. "I'm not sure pink paint was the best choice, Colbie."

"It might not show up as well in the direct sunlight, but it's pretty. That has to count for something. Look at all the volunteers. More just keep arriving." Colbie paused, watching as more team members arrived. Her eyes teared up.

"How is Lil doing?" Honor finished painting a jazzy *R*. "Luke's email this morning said she was still having trouble with her speech."

"Yes, and movement on one side." Colbie gulped, swallowing hard. "I'm having a guilt attack. I feel like I should be with her. What if she needs something?"

"Then Madge will see she gets it," Brooke soothed. "And after this, I'm relieving Madge. It's my shift with Lil, no guilt allowed, got it?"

"Okay, but fair warning." Colbie blew out a shaky sigh and went back to painting. "I'm prone to the guilts."

"No kidding."

Honor spotted Luke's truck pulling into the lot. Sparkles gathered in her stomach. They were sweet and pure and bright, like little pieces of sunshine. Another very ominous sign. When he spotted her and waved, she waved back.

Breezy and casual, remember? She loaded her paintbrush. Laughter and conversation rose from the car washers setting up. How did you stop from feeling? How did you stop from caring?

"He's a really good man." Colbie stood up rotated to the unpainted side of her *A* board and knelt down, paint brush at the ready. "He works hard. He loves his family. He's always there for us whenever we need anything."

"I've noticed." Even she could hear the ring of admiration in her voice. She cleared her throat. Casual, remember? "He's going to make some blessed woman a wonderful husband."

Not me, she wanted to point out, but she was afraid it would give her away.

"Yes, Luke will make a great husband," Brooke enthused. "He's as kind as the day is long. He's loyal. No matter how rough the going gets, he doesn't quit. They don't make many men like him these days."

"And not in California, or at least not that I've found." Not one man—even Kip—had ever made her fill with peace with a single glance. She didn't even know that could happen, like it was happening now. He closed his truck door, settled two sacks of groceries in his arms and tossed a smile her way. Every worry and every doubt faded away, leaving a calm feeling she couldn't deny.

A feeling she wanted to go on forever.

"It's too bad you're heading home soon." Colbie's tone held a questioning note as if there was more she wanted to ask.

"It's definitely too bad I'm leaving in eight days. Seven tomorrow." Counting down used to a great comfort to her. It used to make her feel that her life was still waiting for her, just as she'd left it. Her stomach bunched in a knot. She still wanted to go home, right?

"It sounds like you're rethinking things, maybe?" Brooke asked.

"My life is in Malibu." Friends, family, her church, job applications she'd submitted and there was Anna Louise's wedding to be a part of.

"What's cool about you is that I know you care for Luke." Colbie set down her brush. "No, don't try and deny it. The way you look at him says it all."

"It does." Brooke jumped in, nodding her agreement. "I've noticed it, too."

"Really?" Panic shot through her. Just how transparent had she been? What if Luke suspected how she felt?

"A while back, Luke fell for a woman who worked at his small-town bank. He fell hard for her." Colbie added a few flourishes with her brush. "She led him on, although I'm not sure she meant to. She seemed nice, and I think in all honesty she was lonely and did like him."

"But the minute she'd put in her time as manager, she was able to transfer to Chicago, where she was originally from. With a great big promotion." Brooke shrugged, like she couldn't believe it.

"She never looked back." Colbie stood up, her painting work done. "He'd never admitted it, but Sonya broke Luke's heart."

Poor Luke. She painted an *H* with a flourish. Done.

"No worries," she tried to reassure them. "That won't be a problem this time."

Mainly because Luke didn't have those sorts of feelings for her, and she wouldn't hurt him for anything. Her attention darted to him, where he'd parked his truck and was now carrying grocery sacks to leave with the crowd of car washers. The sun chased him as he headed her way, sending her a grin.

Friendly, not loving. That's how he looked at her as he came up to inspect her *A* board. "Hi, Honor. That's one fine paint job. Unlike Colbie's."

"Hey, I'm no artist." Colbie rolled her eyes. "I should get points for trying."

"It's not so bad," Brooke defended her. "It's better than I could do."

"Just don't put my sign anywhere near Honor's and

no one will know it's lacking." Colbie plopped the lid back on the paint can. "So, what was in the bags?"

"Sodas. Sparkling water. Juice. Paper cups." Luke shrugged as he hefted up the signs, careful of the drying paint. "Figured everyone would get thirsty in this heat. Honor, do you want to help me figure out where to put these?"

"Sure. I'll be happy to offer my opinion." She bounded to her feet, completely nonchalant, as if she *wasn't* effected by him. As if she wasn't falling for him. As if she didn't remember being tucked in his arms, against his iron chest. "How's little Faith doing?"

"Growing like a weed. She's the sweetest thing." He ambled toward the nearby street. "Any chance you could come over and see her one last time before you go? I could throw in a horse riding lesson to tempt you?"

"A horse riding lesson? Where did you ever get the idea I would like to ride a horse?"

"It was implied. Every time I talked about my horse, you seemed interested."

"I was being polite. Honestly." His grin made her knees go weak. Not ideal when she was trying to walk like a perfectly normal person. "Besides, implied is not the same as actual. If I didn't actually say I was interested—"

"But you wouldn't want to meet my horse?"

"Meet, yes. Ride? No."

"Afraid of horses?"

"Sort of and I see no reason to bring that up." She loved the way his laughter matched hers note for note, like melody to harmony. "Besides, I'll be leaving soon. There will be no time. Too bad."

"You don't sound very sorry." He plunked the *A*

board down on the street corner, tugging it to face the busy street. "I was at least hoping for a little sincerity."

"Are you kidding? Give me a surfboard, but a horse? Not so sure about that."

"You surf?" He shook his head. "How did we get to be friends?"

"I was lonely. At the time, I would have settled for anyone." She kept her tone light and cheerful, so he would never guess how her chest squeezed tight. She'd be embarrassed if he knew how she felt. "I was desperate."

"Good thing I came along." He hit the walk button on the light pole. "You could have struck up a friendship with who knows who. Maybe Captain Sweatpants from the chat room."

"It was tempting, even knowing he lived with seven ferrets."

"And his mother," Luke added.

"But I decided to go with Montana Cowboy instead."

"I'm glad, California Girl." The light changed and he stepped off the curb, unaware of how badly she wanted to take his hand, just to feel closer to him. "Your time here is almost up."

"It will go fast." *Now that it is almost here, Lord, please slow down time.* She wanted to find a way to make time last. "I might miss this place."

And you, she'd wanted to say. She would miss him with all her heart.

"Wait one minute. I can't believe my ears. You actually *like* it here?" Luke swung the sign into place on the sidewalk.

"Well, *like* is a strong word," she quipped, fighting to hide the truth. If only she could. "Let's just say

I don't hate it here. I can tolerate not having the ocean near and—"

"—your friends," he finished for her, giving the sign a nudge.

"The problem is that when I go back, I'm going to still miss friends." She swallowed hard to push down the lump building in her throat. "I have friends here I'll have to leave behind."

"No matter where you are, we can still chat online."

"I was talking about your sisters," she quipped, hiding the fact that being online buddies was no longer enough.

Neither was being friends.

So far, so good, Luke thought. He was thankful to the Lord above because Honor had no idea how he felt for her. It was rough hiding his true feelings. He swished the brush in the sudsy bucket, wrung it out and put the final touches on the tire rims. What were the chances she would ever feel that way for him?

Next to nothing. From the first moment her comments online had caught his eye, he'd known she was California-bound. He'd been in this position before with Sonya. He wasn't going to make the same mistake of risking his heart on a woman who never intended to stay, who could never fit into his Montana lifestyle.

"Are you done, Luke?" Colbie broke into his thoughts. She stood, nozzle in hand, ready to rinse down the side of the customer's car.

"You'd better get out of the way," Honor advised sweetly, peeking around the rear bumper of the car she was washing, a mischievous glint in her eye. "I didn't move fast enough last time and Colbie got me."

"Totally accidental." Colbie squeezed, spraying

water so close to him droplets rebounded and splashed his face. "Oops."

"I think someone else should be in charge of the hose." He backed off, swiping his jaw, hardly noticing anything except for the tall, golden-haired beauty who eased in beside him, smelling like sunshine and soap bubbles.

"I volunteer." Honor swiped a froth of soap from her cheek. "Hand it over, Colbie."

"No way. This is too fun. Besides, how else am I going to keep Luke in line?" She squirted down the car, chased soap residue from the tire rims and turned off the nozzle. Her mistake was in putting down the hose.

He caught Honor's eye, winked and snatched it up before anyone could protest.

"The car's looking good." Mr. Paco ambled up to his Cadillac. He owned a local Mexican restaurant. "It hasn't been this clean since it rolled off the showroom floor. I don't get the time to spend on it as much anymore."

"Thanks for stopping in." Luke watched as Colbie and Brandi rubbed down the car, catching every last water droplet. The finish shone in the sun. "We appreciate this more than you know."

"The least I can do for Lil." Mr. Paco sorted through his keys. "Besides, the McKaslins have always been great customers. It's nice to give back. If Lil needs anything, you can call on me. My family is there for you."

"That's why we love you, Mr. Paco." Colbie opened the driver's door for him. "And not only because you make the best nachos in town."

"You kids drop by sometime. The nachos are on me." Mr. Paco settled behind the steering wheel. Colbie shut him in, the engine purred to life and the luxury car ambled off through the church's parking lot.

"Looks like things are wrapping up." Hard to believe the long line of waiting cars was finally gone. Luke felt deeply grateful to the strangers who had stopped in and his fellow church members who had made a point to drive over. Two pails full of cash sat on the table, pails Bree and Brandi were sorting through and tallying up.

"That was fun." Honor grabbed one of the nearby hoses. "Maybe it was the good company."

"No, that can't be it." Good company? No way. Good didn't cut it. Being with her was the best. Even if she hadn't looked at him with a sparkling interest or with gentle affection. His heart could take the disappointment. "I've had better."

Her smile lit her up. That was why he'd said it. He'd do anything to see her smile one more time.

"Hey, Colbie." Mischief glinted in Honor's blue eyes. "I think we forgot something."

"Maybe we did." Colbie, quick on the draw, hefted a second sudsy bucket. "I don't know how we could have missed it."

"Me, either, since it's so obvious."

"As plain as day." Colbie stepped closer.

"And such an eyesore." Honor lifted the nozzle, aiming it at him.

"Don't even think about it. I've got one finger on the trigger." He squeezed, sending a jet of water arcing from the hose he held on to the pavement in front of Honor's feet. "A warning shot."

"It's two against one." Honor yanked the hose closer. "Colbie, I'll cover you. Grab another hose."

"Colbie, if you move," Luke cautioned, "I'll take you down."

"You do it, and I'll be merciless." Laughing, Honor sent a shot of water his way, except she must have misjudged because a hard stream jetted him right in the face. The girls dissolved into giggles. "Sorry. I thought it was set on sprinkle."

"It doesn't matter." He swiped water from his eyes with his free hand. "This means war."

"No!" Honor shrieked, laughing too hard to dart away when he turned the nozzle on her. Water sluiced through the air, drenching her.

But she wasn't without defensive skills. She trained her hose on him. He ignored the blast of water, moving in, sprinkling her with the fresh, cool water. It felt good in the blazing heat with the sunshine smiling over them. Through the glistening water droplets and Honor's lilting laughter, her gaze met his that was for one second unguarded. He felt closer to her than to anyone.

Then he tripped over a speed bump, went down on his knee and the hose jumped out of his hand. He was fine, nothing was hurt, but her concern made him see something he'd never let himself acknowledge before.

"Are you all right?" She knelt down beside him. Her touch to his arm felt as warm as heaven.

Love brimmed his soul, simple and sweet.

"I'm fine. You let your guard down." In more ways than one. He'd seen straight into her heart. Filled with hope, he stole the hose from her. "Whoops."

"Hey!" She didn't have time to protest because a stream of refreshing, cool water poured over him from behind.

"Don't worry, Honor. I've got your back." Colbie held the third hose, proudly pointing it over his head.

"Colbie? How could you turn on me like this? At least Honor—"

"Oops." Honor's hand closed over his and turned his own nozzle into his chest. Water shot off his shirt, spewed into his face and he sputtered, overpowered but not without hope.

Chapter Thirteen

"How's the reading going?" Days later, Honor hunkered down on the chair across from her student. The crinkle of leather echoed in the library's stillness. "Steinbeck isn't too boring, right?"

"I guess." Jerrod looked up from his book. "The good part is by this time next week, I'll be on a plane heading for California."

"Don't rub it in. If only I could say the same." She winked, glad for the kid.

"A word of advice. Mom goes over the rooms with her eagle eye. Don't think if there's a speck of dust or a nail hole she won't take it out of your last paycheck." Jerrod shook his head. "I'm just sayin'."

"Thanks for the warning. I'll be extra thorough. You're going to do well on the exam. You've put in the work."

"My parents will be happy." He shrugged. "I just wanted them to be happy together, you know?"

"I do." Relationships weren't always what you hoped they could be. Neither were people. "Your parents have made their decision. I just wish it was easier on you."

"At least I'll get to stay with Dad the rest of the summer. I'm done with Montana."

"I know just how you feel." The words tumbled out from habit, because that's how she'd felt the instant she'd driven across the California state line.

Except it was no longer true.

"It's officially five o'clock." She pushed off the chair. It was Friday afternoon. Only one week to go. "Time to quit."

"Then I'm outta here!" Jerrod tossed aside his book and darted straight to the door, leaving her alone in the silent room.

Her cell chimed with a text message. She brightened seeing Luke's name. R U done 4 the day? he'd written.

Done. Where R U?

Sitting at the gate.

He was here! Just like he'd promised. She skipped out of the room and was halfway down the hall before she realized what she was doing. *Skipping, honestly? You know he's the wrong man,* she thought. *So why are you feeling this way?*

Because she couldn't help it. The answer was obvious the moment she spotted his truck ambling up the drive, pulling a horse trailer.

Okay, the horse trailer was a surprise. She hopped down the front steps. Hadn't he said he'd be coming with a thank-you dinner for helping at Lil's fundraiser? She mentally went through the emails he'd written her over the past two days, but she couldn't remember a thing about why he would drive all this way with a horse.

"Oh, he's the one you've been rushing off to see." Wren stood in the open doorway, leaning against the frame, the hem of her apron ruffling in the breeze. "I can see why. He's a total hunk."

"It's not like that." Boy, was her tone defensive, or what?

"Then what it is like?" Wren nodded knowingly. "If that man were interested in me, I would give him a chance."

"He's not interested in me." And wasn't that a knife to her heart?

"He drove all this way to see you. A man doesn't do that if he's not interested." Wren leaned backward, listening and winced. "Mrs. Lambert calls. I gotta go. Have fun."

Fun? With Luke that was guaranteed. She flew off the stairs and breezed up the walkway, his presence drawing her toward him. She'd lost all ability to resist the pull.

"Hey, there." The truck door slammed and Luke circled into view, striking in a gray T-shirt and jeans. His Stetson shaded his face, emphasizing the rugged strength of his square jaw.

Yep, totally hunky. No doubt about it. "Wow, you're right on time. What's with the horse trailer?"

"That would be one of the surprises I have in store. Beware."

"I'm learning I have to keep an eye on you."

"Good idea. You never know what I'm gonna do." He swept her into his arms in a welcome hug. He was sun-warm and smelled good, like hay and summer sun. He released her before she had a chance to settle in against his wonderful chest. *That was too bad,* she thought as she stumbled onto the concrete, unable to breathe.

I wish, she thought. *If only he felt the same way for me.*

"I'm glad we planned this." He knuckled back his hat. "I've got dinner packed in my saddlebags. How does that sound?"

"Saddlebags? I thought we'd be eating at my place, or maybe we'd go in search of a restaurant?"

"Not even close. Don't worry. I know how to do up Friday evening."

"With a horse?"

"Horses."

"As in plural?"

"Roger that. Come with me."

"I'm not sure I should."

"Why not?" He reached up and lowered a metallic ramp from the back of the trailer. "I checked ahead. There are riding trails through the forest. I'm assuming those stables over there used to hold horses."

"The previous owners must have been riders." *Certainly not Mrs. Lambert,* she thought, *and absolutely not me.*

"Come meet Buck." He disappeared into the trailer.

"Buck? Your horse's name is *Buck,* as in he bucks people off?"

"Buck as in Buckwheat." Luke's laughter rumbled as merry as the sunshine, echoing inside the trailer.

She didn't even remember taking a step yet there she was, peering into the trailer. Two horses stood patiently, nose in, their tales swishing. Luke stood next to the brown horse, his touch gentle and his movements sure. He looked beyond comfortable around the animals. Too bad she couldn't say the same.

"Is this a bad time to confess something?" she asked.

"Like what?"

"That I'm a tiny bit scared of horses?"

"Seriously? You couldn't have mentioned that at any-time in at least one email you've sent me during the last few months?"

"It didn't come up." Wow, those horses looked big in real life. Huge. Ginormous. Colossal. "When you mentioned a riding lesson I didn't think you really meant it."

"You were hoping I didn't." Humor brought out his dimples. "You may have figured I'm like most men. Men say a lot but follow through very little."

"Let's just say I never imagined you would drive your horses all this way." She stepped aside as the brown horse backed flawlessly down the ramp and into the sunshine, where he gleamed a rich nut-brown. His inky mane and tail rippled in the wind and he pawed the ground, tossing his head and nickering low in his throat, his big chocolate eyes watching Luke intently.

"Here you go, buddy." Luke held out his hand and the horse lipped up the molasses treat with his velvety lips.

Okay, as long as she kept a safe distance from the creature, he really was magnificent. *The horse,* she told herself firmly, *not the man.*

Okay, fine. The man was magnificent, too. Why couldn't she stop noticing? What were the chances she would suddenly be able to find him ugly? That would solve her problems very nicely.

"Here. Hold him for me." Luke thrust the reins in her direction.

"But—" She didn't have a chance to protest. Her fingers curled around the leather straps and Luke disappeared inside the trailer, leaving her face-to-face with a horse.

Equine eyes stared into hers. A horsy brow quirked.

What did she do? Say hello? Quirk her brow, too? Hope he didn't bite?

Buck snorted out his rather big nostrils.

At least his snort sort of sounded friendly. Maybe he, like his master, just wanted to be friends.

"You're really enormous," she felt obliged to inform the animal. "Horses look smaller when they're grazing in some field."

Buck studied her for a moment, lifted his head and his whiskery lips nibbled across her forehead.

Not being a fool, she jumped back. Buck just kept coming. She stepped back. He stepped forward.

"Uh, Luke?" Eventually she was going to run out of driveway. "Help?"

"Don't worry. He won't hurt you." Boots knelled on the metal ramp as he walked the second horse down to the pavement. Not that she could see him because Buck's enormous body blocked all view of Luke.

"You also have really big teeth." She could see them as the animal's velvety mouth brushed her forehead. Oh, so he was trying to kiss her. She laughed, since the joke had been on her. "That tickles."

Buck's eyes brightened happily. He nickered, lowered his head and waited. She couldn't resist the invitation. She stroked her fingertips down the long slope of his nose. His coat was short and bristly and amazing.

"He's pretty great, huh?" Luke sidled in, holding a set of reins and petting the second horse's nose.

"Totally great." She wasn't just talking about Buck. Actually, she wasn't talking about him at all.

"Let's get these horses saddled and we'll get on with our ride. I've packed you a picnic you won't soon forget."

"That sounds a little ambiguous. Why won't I forget it? Because it will be so bad? Or so good?"

"I'll never tell. It's a mystery. I'll let you figure it out for yourself."

"You know I like a good mystery," she quipped, thinking of the book they'd been discussing in the chat room where she'd first "met" Montana cowboy.

Maybe he wasn't the wrong man at all, she thought. The trouble might be she was the wrong woman—the wrong woman for him.

Luke checked Buck's cinch. Tight enough. He patted the gelding's sun-warmed neck, doing his level best not to second guess his decision. He had to put his heart on the line. He cared about Honor too much not to try. He couldn't take his eyes off her. In jeans, a summery top and with her hair in a ponytail, she'd never looked prettier as she did petting the white mare's nose.

"You're right. Lena is as gentle as a lamb. Okay. I'll give it a try."

"This might not be a stroll along the beach, but a trail ride is great, too. Trust me."

"Trust you? Hmm, I'm not sure I should."

"Hey, I'm trustworthy."

"So you say." Mischief glinted in shades of blue as she met his gaze. "I like new adventures, but I'm not fond of falling."

"Don't worry. It won't hurt until you hit the ground."

"Oh, that helps."

He liked to hear her laugh. "Hop on up."

"Lena, are you going to be good to me?" Woman looked horse in the eye. The mare nodded, tossing her mane, and the woman smiled.

Then, when her smile deepened as he caught her hand, it gave him reassurance. "Hand on the saddle horn. Boot in the stirrup, and lift yourself up. It's that simple."

She rose up into the air and landed with a light plop in the saddle. "Wow. So far, so good."

"See? I'll make a Montana girl out of you yet."

"You go ahead and try, cowboy." She plucked the reins from the pommel and held onto the saddle horn tightly with her free hand. "I'd still rather be sailing."

"Famous last words." He patted Lena on the shoulder before gathering Buck's reins and mounting up. Buck shifted beneath him, already moving. "Prepare yourself for some Montana fun."

"Would this be a good or bad time to tell you I'm not fond of the forest?"

He couldn't tell if she was kidding him or not. He sidled Buck alongside Lena. "What's there not to like about the forest?"

"Well, for one thing, bugs."

"Bugs? That's what you're worried about?"

"Big hairy spiders. Creepy crawling things with a hundred legs. Mosquitoes that suck your blood."

"Wow, your wild imagination is kinda scary. Tell you what. If a big hairy leggy bug comes along, I'll bat him away. Or flick him off your hair."

"That's not helping."

"It's really not the bugs you have to worry about." He reined Buck toward the edge of the tree line, where a path carved its way between tall pines. "It's the snakes."

"What? Why did you have to bring that up?" Her blue eyes laughed at him, her grip tightening around the saddle horn until her knuckles were white.

"Full disclosure. There's also bear, cougar and moose. They can be aggressive and hungry."

"I'm so comforted now."

"Glad I could help." He stayed at her side, keeping an eye on gentle Lena, who walked along at an easy clip. Honor stayed in her saddle, straight and tall, as if she were born to ride.

"I know what you're doing." She arched a brow, shooting him a sideways look.

"Uh, would that be trying to lower your expectations so you aren't disappointed in the evening's activity?"

"No, you're keeping my mind off the fact that I'm lurching and sliding around on the back of a horse."

"Is it working?"

"Slightly."

But it *was* working. That's what mattered. Fine, so he was hoping to change her mind about the Montana wilderness. He was hoping she fell in love with horseback riding, and that he had a chance with her heart. He knuckled back his hat so he could see her better.

Do I have a shot, Lord? he asked. *Is there a chance?* When he opened his eyes, he was rewarded by the sight of her. Honey hair tousled by the wind, ivory skin aglow and sliding a little in the saddle. "Are you okay there? Grip with your knees."

"Easy for you to say. You call this fun?"

"Just wait. You'll see."

"Okay. How long should I wait? Oops!" She laughed when Lena lunged into a cantor, the horse taking advantage of her green rider. "Uh oh! Now what do I do?"

"Hold on tight."

"That's the advice you give me? Some instructor you are."

The mare gave a horsy trumpet of challenge, Buck answered and leaped into a gallop. He let the horse have some fun, zipping along with Lena down the sun-dappled trail. Honor's laughter lifting on the wind told him she was having fun. So was he.

"Are you staying on okay?" he asked, since she was listing to the left.

"This is sort of like surfing. It takes a while to get the hang of it. But I learned how to stay on the board, I can figure out how to stay in a saddle. *I think*."

"Go ahead and ease back on the reins if you want her to slow down." Why wasn't he surprised when she didn't? Woman and horse barreled down the pathway, leaping ahead of him and Buck, tail and ponytail waving in the slipstream.

"Hey, I'm starting to get the hang of this!" she called over her shoulder. "This really is fun!"

He saw disaster an instant before it happened. A blur of movement in his peripheral vision, the teenager's shout of surprise and the horse's alarmed whinny had him launching off the saddle before Buck could fully stop. He hit the ground so hard, the impact jarred his bones and nearly knocked him to his knees. But Honor hadn't fallen. Lena had stopped in time.

"Is everyone all right?" Adrenaline roared through him, since for one instant he'd been haunted by the image of Honor falling and hitting the ground. He blinked twice, just to make sure she was still in the saddle.

"That was a close one." Jerrod rolled onto his feet, stood and dusted dirt from his knees. "I didn't know you'd be out here on a horse, Honor. I thought you didn't like horses."

"It's true, I usually avoid them. Shouldn't you be going the other way? I thought you would be long gone by now." Honor patted Lena's neck, soothing the horse.

"I forgot my sunglasses. Don't worry. Not the first

time I've bit the dust." Jerrod grabbed his fallen bike by the handlebars. "Luke, I like your horses."

"Thanks. Looks like Lena likes you."

"Sorry about that, girl." The teen rubbed the horse's nose. "Well, I gotta scoot. See ya, Honor."

"Have fun." She was grateful the horse didn't seem afraid of the boy or the bike as they passed by, riding out of sight. She let her hand rest on Lena's neck, loving the warm, alive feel of the animal beneath her palm.

"For a minute there, I thought you might hit the dust, too." Luke's hand settled on her knee, gazing up at her. "Was afraid I couldn't get to you fast enough."

"I managed to hold on. Lena was great. She hardly startled when Jerrod came racing around the corner." She gave the horse another pat. "And you! I've never seen anyone move so fast."

"I wanted to catch you if I could."

"It's nice knowing you wouldn't have let me fall." Okay, her feelings had gone too far to try to call them back. Affection whispered through her as sweet as a Sunday hymn. It shone in his eyes, too. Encouraged, she straightened in her saddle. The dappled sunshine, the hot puff of wind and the man beside her could not have been more perfect.

"Guess I'd better mount up." Luke shook his head as Buck moved in to nibble at his hat brim. "All right, we'll get moving, big fella. I think he's been looking forward to this as much as I have."

Me most of all, she thought as he mounted up. Impossible to look away from the man. She was not ready for the perils of romance, but her heart was taking her on a journey, one she didn't want to miss. She gathered the reins, grabbed hold of the saddle horn for good measure and let Lena carry her down the trail.

* * *

"You're getting a little pink from the sun." Luke swung down from Buck in the shady cove. They had been riding for over an hour to reach this spot. The sparkling surface of the mountain lake added to the tranquil scenery as the cowboy paced toward her, sweeping off his hat. "Here. This ought to help."

"It's too big." The Stetson slipped over her head with plenty of room to spare, sliding down to cut off her view of him.

"Sure, that's because I have a big head, or so my brother tells me, because it's full of hot air." He knuckled back the brim for her. "Or so Hunter keeps telling me."

"That was my first opinion of you."

"That's what all the ladies say. I never impress 'em. Right, Lena?"

The mare nosed in, drawn by the merry conversation. Luke rubbed the horse's nose. Strong man.

Gentle heart.

That's what roped her in and held her there, refusing to let her go.

"Yes, that's exactly what your sisters have told me. Warned me about, actually." She knelt down and chose a pebble from the shore. "You have one flaw after another."

"True. I can't deny it." He unbuckled packs from the back of Buck's saddle. "My faults are hard to miss."

"You're always there for your family."

"I suppose I *could* try to be there less."

"You work hard." She gave the stone a toss. It bounced three times on the mirrored surface.

"I could try to be lazy. Sit around more. Maybe let my bills go past due." He shook out a table cloth to spread over the wild grasses. "And what about you? No work ethic whatsoever."

"Right." The wind snatched a corner of the cloth and she knelt to catch it. "I also am a pretty good aim with a garden hose."

"I remember. A definite flaw." He shouldered the packs onto the cloth and settled down. "I got completely drenched. I'll never trust you at a car wash again."

"We had fun." She eased onto the ground, the big blue checked cloth protecting her from any haphazardly crawling bugs. "I always have a good time with you."

"Go on, I like hearing compliments."

"Sure, since you probably don't hear them often."

"Not ever. How did you know?" His baritone rumbled with amusement as he opened the packs. Delicious scents of fried chicken, buttermilk biscuits and macaroni salad filled the air.

Overwhelming contentment filled her. She'd never been so happy. Not even in California. Not with her friends. She breathed in the serenity of the lake, the beauty of the scenery and knew the reason she saw Montana differently, and he was sitting right in front of her.

Chapter Fourteen

The sun dimmed halfway through their picnic. Thunderheads sailed from the southwest, blotting out half of the robin's egg sky. *Let's hope those clouds keep going,* Luke thought as he bit into a biscuit.

"The thing I like about Montana is the wide, endless sky." Honor pulled a piece of crispy skin off a drumstick and popped it into her mouth. "It goes on forever."

"Just like the ocean?"

"Exactly. It's peaceful here, too. I hadn't realized. It's the same feeling I get standing on the shore with the water lapping over my feet."

"I know that feeling. Like everything is bigger than you. Larger than life. It fills you with wonder at the greatness of God's creation."

"Yes, that's it. I thought nothing could do that better than the ocean at sunset, but this comes close to equaling it." She breathed in the fresh air, looking content, looking like a woman who belonged in this moment, in this meadow with him. "The evening light on those mountains takes my breath away."

"Me, too." Except he wasn't looking at the mountains. Just her. Only at her. "Did I hear you right? Montana is almost equaling California in your view?"

"Almost. Shocked, aren't you? Never thought I'd say such a thing, did you? Me, either, but this forest really is beautiful, and no bugs so far. Those mountains are incredible. They'd be great to ski."

That surprised him. "You ski?"

"Downhill and cross-country."

"Me, too." He broke off a hunk of biscuit, thinking it over. "Could be you're starting to fit in here?"

"Could be."

But was it enough to stay? he wondered. He could only hope so. "Maybe you'll have to come back to visit this winter. I'll take you skiing and promise you the time of your life."

"It always is when I'm with you." The truth shone in her eyes like a secret only he could see.

His heart beat double-time with hope stronger than any he'd known. He wanted things to change between them. This evening, he intended to let her know about the deep, abiding affection he felt for her. An affection that strengthened day by day. An affection nothing could stop. He picked a wildflower and slipped it into the hair folded behind her ear. Her hair felt like satin against his fingers, her skin like silk.

"Nice." She smiled up at him, the buttercup tucked in place, yellow petals against sunshine gold.

Tell her, he thought. *Just do it. Let her know how you feel.*

"I—" That's as far as he got. The sky split open and rain pelted to the ground like liquid bullets.

"That came out of nowhere fast." She hurried to toss lids on the food containers. Only then did he realize the sunshine had vanished.

"Welcome to Montana." At least the meal was mostly over. He launched to rescue a canister. "I've got dessert. Hurry."

"At least you know what's important." She seized his outstretched hand and raced with him through the rain-soaked grass. "I see blue skies over there."

"It's just a squall. It'll pass." He found a protected spot beneath the boughs and shouldered in. "Don't worry. I'm checking for spiders."

"Whew." She tumbled in after him. Rainwater sluiced down her nose. Her hair dripped water, too, darkened to a honey-shade. She bumped against his chest, nestling into the shelter. "You're a keeper, Luke. And you saved the cookies."

"Hey, I know what's important."

Droplets ricocheted off the ground, plopped off branches and dripped on the horses who nosed into the trees they'd been tethered to, unconcerned and grazing.

"I can't catch a break." He chuckled, shook his head, sending droplets flying. "You think a picnic in the middle of summer would be safe from rainstorms."

"You couldn't have planned it better. I love rain."

"I thought you loved the sun."

"I do, but there's nothing quite like a rainstorm." Quite possibly there was nothing like being tucked beneath cedar boughs with Luke. The smell of rain, the electric charge in the air and the affection warm in her soul.

There had been a story she'd meant to tell him about the rainstorms along the beach, but she couldn't seem to remember exactly what she'd intended to say. Her brain cells had ceased to function. Probably it was from being snuggled cozily against him, wet and warm from the rain, laughing and breathless from the run to the trees. The only thing she could think about was him.

He wasn't like any man she'd ever met. No slick, practiced lines. No driving ambition. He was solid as the earth, the kind of guy who would never let a woman down. Exactly the man she would want to weather any storm alongside.

"I'm the same way. Whatever season I'm in, whatever weather I'm in, it's my favorite." He gestured toward the roiling black clouds overhead. "There's a good side and a down side to everything. The trick is to enjoy the good side because things change. That's life, always changing."

"Right." She couldn't concentrate on what he was saying. His chest was steely solid and she knew exactly what it felt to lean her cheek against his shirt. If only he would fold his strong arms around her again. Their gazes met. Could he see what she wanted? Could he guess how she felt? She didn't think she could hide it any longer. Her feelings shone brightly, even in the storm's darkness.

"Life changing, that's the one thing you can count on." He leaned in, closer. "Sometimes you have to seize the moment."

"Y-yes." She stuttered, forgetting how to talk and how to breath because his callused fingertips grazed her cheek. Tender. Gentle. Electric.

Her pulse flatlined. He leaned in closer yet. This was it. He was going to kiss her. Nerves popped in her stomach but she didn't move away. Not in a thousand years. This was everything she'd ever wanted. She tilted up to meet his kiss. Nothing, not one thing, was more tender than the brush of his lips to hers.

Sweet. Love spiraled through her quietly, joyfully.

She clung to him, savoring the closeness. When he broke the kiss, she felt dizzy. Disoriented. The only thing steadying her was his arms as he drew her against his chest.

The only place she ever wanted to be.

While he held her, the rain overhead eased. Fast-moving clouds took the rain cell over the lake, turning the water to pewter. Sun broke out from above, casting a rainbow through a slice of blue sky.

Her cell rang, startling her. "I have service out here?"

"There's a town and probably a cell tower on the north shore of the lake. Probably can't see it from here." He led the way out from beneath the tree now that the coast was clear. "Go ahead and answer it. I'll start packing up."

"Don't you need help?"

"I've got it. Talk to your friends." He tossed her a dazzling smile before he strode away to check on the horses. Her heart beat faster remembering his kiss.

His kiss! It made her feel floaty, but, no, her feet really were touching the ground. "Hello?"

"It's me." Kelsey's voice practically vibrated with excitement. "I've got news."

"It sounds like good news." She couldn't stop smiling, either. A brand-new possibility for her life had opened up with Luke's kiss. A possibility she wanted more than anything. "What's going on with you? Tell me."

"It's not my news. It's yours. I just got home and found a message on the machine. I don't know why they called here and not your cell, but you've been offered a job."

"A teaching job?"

"Yes! With your old school. A history teacher is

going on maternity leave and they are offering you her position. Isn't that great? When you come home, you're here to stay. We've got a party lined up to celebrate. Big-time. Chocolate cake. Balloons. We'll have a blast."

"A job." Why did she feel so let down? This should be good news, right? "I've been offered a job at Wheatly."

"Isn't that what I just said? I'm totally jazzed." Kelsey squealed. "I'm doing a Snoopy dance."

"Me, too." Except she wasn't squealing. She wasn't Snoopy dancing. She was crestfallen. Why did her dream job have to come through now? The chance to teach again at the Wheatly Academy was a miracle in itself.

"I gotta go. I've got a date." Kelsey's voice vibrated with excitement.

"A date?" That was news. "Okay, there's a lot you're not telling me."

"Now's not the time, as there isn't any time. I still have to do my hair. But Dom is really great. A total gentleman. He could be The One!"

"That's great, Kels. Have a good time." After saying their goodbyes, she pocketed her phone, more than a little stunned.

"Hey, is everything all right?" Luke slung a saddlebag over his shoulder. "You look a little shell-shocked."

"I'm just surprised how life can turn on a dime."

"I thought we agreed that's life, always changing. Not much stays the same." He held out a container. "All that and we didn't get dessert. How about a cookie?"

"That should help." Damp hung in the air, but the bold sun kept her warm. Birds sang as she took one of the iced cookies from the container. Off in the distance the storm cloud swept across the lake, heading northeast. The rainbow had disappeared. "I just got some surprising news."

"Is everything okay back home?" He took a cookie for himself and stowed the container in a saddlebag.

"Yes. Everything's fine." She looked at the cookie as if she wasn't sure she wanted to take a bite. "You know the school I used to work for?"

"Where you also substituted for a while after your job was cut?"

"That's the one. A position has opened up for September and they've invited me to fill it."

"Is that so?" He eased the pack behind Buck's saddle, glad she couldn't see the look on his face. He'd really gotten his hopes up. Way up there. They hit the ground with a crash. "Sounds like good news to me. Congratulations."

"Thanks. It's exactly what I've been praying for."

"Me, too. This is good for you." He squared his shoulders, facing her. "I want you to be happy."

"I guess I'm still in shock."

"Good things happen to those who wait." A dumb thing to say, but it was the best he could do. His fingers shook so badly he could barely buckle the saddlebag into place. For a moment there, he'd been convinced he had a chance with her. That kiss…

He shook his head. That kiss had been a stolen moment between them. But a future with her?

It clearly was not meant to be. God's plan for her wouldn't keep her in Montana.

Which meant he had to let her go. "Hey, you'll be able to see Jerrod, assuming he aces his test and gets into Wheatly."

"Right. I may even be his teacher again." She brightened, nibbling on her cookie and confirming his suspicion.

She intended to accept the offer. Once back in Malibu with her friends and at the school she loved, she wouldn't be spending much time online. Her life would be full. There would be no room for him.

Boy, he was gonna miss her.

He drew Lena's reins and held the mare for mounting. "You probably can't wait to get back."

"Oh, I'm in no hurry. For instance, I've having a lovely time tonight." She tossed him a smile as she swept into the saddle.

Her smile held him captive. The most beautiful one he'd ever seen. He held the mare steady, careful to give nothing away. "Even with the rain? It put a damper on things."

"No, not unless we both went back and sat on the ground."

"You're right. That would be a damper. Ha ha." He handed up her reins. She could warm away any letdown. She could have been his entire world. "Ready to head back?"

"Might as well. There are more thunderheads coming this way." She tilted her head back to study the sky, one hand on his hat she still wore. "They look ominous."

"We don't want to be caught in the forest if lightning decides to strike." He grabbed Buck's reins. "That would be a shocking experience."

"Really? That's a terrible pun." Honor nosed Lena around to face the trail.

"It would give us a jolt." He mounted up. "Light up the evening."

"Honestly. Your puns are funnier when you're typing

them." Mischief sparkled as she led the way along the trail. "This has been fun. Much more than I figured."

"Good. Then you admit it. You like horseback riding?"

"I totally get it. I really do." She leaned forward in her saddle to pat Lena's neck. "Horses are incredibly cool."

"I've always thought so." This time it was his cell that interrupted. A text message from Colbie. He squinted at the screen. "Looks like its official. Lil is going home tomorrow."

"What a relief Lil is doing so well."

"She'll do even better at home." He didn't mention the challenges ahead. "Like I've told you in more than a few emails, I'm grateful we didn't lose her. Not sure what we would all do without our Lil."

"She's your mom."

He liked that Honor understood. Sometimes family wasn't made of blood ties but by bonds of the heart that were as equally strong. He reined Buck down the sloping trail, listening to the flurry of birds rushing about. Sounded like they were seeking shelter, which meant another storm was on the way. As he glanced through the canopy of trees, the sky looked progressively darker with each passing minute.

They reached the Lamberts' property before the first flash of lightning snaked across the sky. He'd unsaddled both horses and had only Buck to load in the trailer when the next round of raindrops hit. All he could think about was their kiss. The tenderness he felt for Honor refused to budge as he patted Buck's flank, turned on his heel and put up the ramp.

Honor stood in the rain, arms wrapped around her middle, watching him quietly. Was she thinking about their kiss, too? Regretting it, maybe? Or was she thinking it was a sweet end to their relationship? His throat bunched up as he walked her way.

"Looks like we're in for more than a squall." Easy to talk about the weather. Talking about his feelings was another matter. "The weathermen were wrong."

"Again." Her smile held sadness, although the Stetson she still wore shaded her face, hiding her eyes from him. "What's a picnic without a little rain?"

"Boring, that's what." He knuckled back the hat to get a better look at her. What if this was the last time he ever saw her?

"I had no idea you were such a good cook. I would have figured a Montana cowboy for the kind of man who's too rugged to spend time in a kitchen."

"Once Hunter and I were on our own, we had to figure something out or starve." It was tough keeping his tone light, as if this wasn't killing him. Letting her go was the hardest thing he'd ever done. The only reason he could do it was simple. It was what she wanted. "Something had to be done, so I stepped up and figured it out. Good thing for the cooking channel. That's how I learned."

"Wow, well that was the best fried chicken I'd ever had. You're a man of many talents, Luke McKaslin."

"You know what they say. A jack of all trades, a master at none."

"Yeah, right." She shook her head. "I don't believe that for a second. Thank you for driving all this way—"

"—it was my pleasure, ma'am."

"And for a memorable evening. I'll never forget it."

"Neither will I."

"This is a remarkable turning point for me. I actually like Montana now."

"Just in time to leave." He eased in a step closer.

"It's ironic." How did she tell him that part of it had to do with him? Maybe it wasn't where you were, but who you were with that mattered. "I'm part Montana girl now, thanks to you."

"Glad I could help. I think Buck and Lena played a role." Affection warmed his words.

And made her wish for another kiss. She had no idea what to do about her job offer, but she knew one thing. The man standing before her was all she wanted. He was all she could see. Not the rain, not stormy skies, just his strength and character, the man who had stolen her heart.

"Yes, Lena definitely made the difference." She couldn't say what she felt. It was too great. "It was the horses. They changed my mind."

"Horses can do that. They're pretty awesome."

"No argument." The future flashed into her mind, a wish for what could be. Evenings spent with him, easy banter and tenderness. He was everything she'd ever wanted and never believed she could find. What was a job compared to that? Her heart had already chosen.

What she didn't know is if he would choose her.

"I'd best get on the road." Instead of reaching out like she hoped, Luke stepped back. "I promised to drop by the hospital and check on Lil on the way home."

"With the horses?"

"It won't take more than a few extra minutes out of the way. They're comfortable in the trailer. I just want to see her with my own eyes. Make sure she's good." He hesitated, staying rooted to the ground, still not moving in for a goodbye kiss. "There will be a lot to do over the weekend getting her settled."

"I could help."

"I appreciate that, but you've done so much already. Besides, you'll want to get started packing, right?" Sadness darkened his eyes to a deep violet-blue. "You're homeward bound."

"Y-yes." She stumbled over the word. "Yes, I am."

"You're getting soaked to the skin standing out here." He pulled his keys from his pocket. "Go on, get inside and dry off. Thanks for hanging with me this evening."

"It was f-fun." That wasn't the word she'd wanted to use. Amazing. Illuminating. It could have been life-changing. Had she been wrong about their kiss? Maybe it hadn't been as meaningful for him as it had for her, she realized, as Luke simply walked away.

Like the friend he'd always been. A friend, nothing more.

Heartbreak came quietly, like the stillness after a storm breaks. "Wait, don't forget your hat."

"Keep it." He tugged open his truck door. "It looks good on you."

For one moment, what looked like regret and heartbreak flashed in his eyes. In another blink it was gone. Whatever his feelings for her, they were not strong enough to ask her to stay.

"Have a safe drive." She choked on the words. "Give Lil my l-love."

"Will do." He swung up behind the wheel. "I'll email you. I suspect my sisters will want to throw you a big going away bash."

"Great. You know I love a party. Because of the—"

"—cake," he finished. He closed the door, and that was the end of all possibility. The engine turned over, the truck rumbled as it pulled away and the last she saw of him was his hand waving out the open window.

She waited until the truck was out of sight before

sinking to her knees. Her heart shattered into a thousand pieces, never to be put right again. That's how she felt without him.

And always would.

Lord, I know I handled that the right way, he prayed as he punched the elevator button. *But it doesn't feel right.*

No answer came as the doors clunked shut. The compartment stuttered upward, jerking just enough to make him wish he'd taken the stairs. The hospital was quiet this time of evening, right before visiting hours ended. His boots knelled against the floor and echoed against the walls as he wound his way through the corridors.

He'd been troubled ever since he'd left Honor standing in the rain. Her image framed in his side view mirror seemed burned in his brain. He couldn't forget how forlorn she looked, hugging herself with his hat hiding part of her face. She was everything he wanted. Every little piece of his heart.

"Mom's sleeping." Colbie eased out of the bedside chair and padded over to him. "She's looking better, don't you think?"

"Her color is better." He leaned one shoulder against the doorjamb. Lil lay peacefully on her back, so slight and frail she was barely a bump beneath the covers. He swallowed hard. "She doesn't look strong enough to be moved."

"She can't wait to go home. She wrote it down so I couldn't argue with her. It will be better for her to recover where she's more comfortable. She hates hospitals."

"I'll bring my second TV when I come back in the

morning. I'll set it up in her bedroom, so she can keep up with her shows."

"She'll love that." Colbie squeezed his arm, concern lining her face. "Are you all right?"

"I have to be." He didn't say anything more. Let his sister think he was still hurting over Lil. That was true, too. But there was a break in his heart that would never heal.

Honor was leaving. He'd always known she would. But he'd never bargained on his feelings deepening this much. He would give anything to have her stay, but why would she? She had everything she wanted waiting for her back in Malibu. Asking her to stay would just complicate matters and mess up their friendship. Their friendship was all he really had of her, for however long it lasted.

"I have the horses in the trailer, so I'd better get going." He took off before Colbie could question him about his evening out with Honor. "Call if you need anything."

"Will do. See you tomorrow." Colbie, bless her, didn't say anything more, although he could feel the weight of her gaze on his back as he hurried down the hall. Chances were she'd figured it all out, anyway. Country boy and city girl. Anyone could see how they'd never been meant to be right from the start.

He'd known it, but that didn't stop him from wishing. It didn't stop him from loving her.

Chapter Fifteen

Honor couldn't believe how fast her last week at the Lamberts' whizzed by. She glanced into her rearview mirror for a quick check and then concentrated on the road ahead of her. Her eyes were tired from the long drive, and it wasn't over yet. She'd left the Lambert compound with her car packed and her job done. Right now Jerrod and Olive were headed to the airport to catch a flight. His exam was bright and early Monday morning.

And she should be celebrating and jumping for joy. Isn't this what she'd been waiting for? But the entire time she'd spent packing, cleaning her apartment above the garage and fitting her suitcases into her car, she hadn't been upbeat. Not once. Sadness set in hard. Tomorrow she would start her drive home. This was her final day in Montana.

A day spent with Luke. His sisters were throwing a going away party for her. How nice was that? Her biggest problem was being face-to-face with Luke.

I can do this. She gripped her steering wheel more tightly and for good measure added a prayer. *Lord, help me get through this.*

What she needed was a good strategy. Act like he hadn't stolen her heart. Pretend she wasn't in love with him. Forget their kiss that had haunted her through the last week of her job.

Her cell rang as she slowed on the outskirts of Prospect, Montana. The small rural town near Luke's ranch looked like something out of a movie with its tidy main street, bright awnings and a hitching post in front of the feed store. She didn't have to look at her display to know who was on the line. "Hi, Luke."

"Just wanted to make sure you weren't lost." He sounded wonderful. It was so good to hear his voice.

"I'm following your directions just fine. I printed out the email and have it in case I wind up in Canada."

"Where are you now?"

"Heading down Main. I'm just passing the diner."

"The grocery store is a block on your right. Turn in and come join me, if you want. I'm here picking out potato chips."

"You'd better have barbecue chips in your cart."

"The first bag I chose." Humor warmed his words. "I know they're your favorite."

"You're a good friend." That word cost her. It rolled off her tongue, but it hurt. It would always hurt. "A friend never lets another down in the chip aisle."

"That's the true measure." A crinkle sounded in the background. "Sour cream and onion for Hunter."

"It does sound like you could use help." She signaled and rolled into the parking lot. "How many bags are you getting?"

"Everyone has a favorite."

"Hold on. I'll be right there." She swung into an empty spot beside Luke's truck in the mostly empty lot and turned off the engine.

I can do this, she told herself again, bolstering her courage. *Just be light and breezy. Casual. You've done it before, you can do it again.* All she had to do was make it through the afternoon without Luke ever guessing how hard she'd fallen for him. That's it, nothing more. She could do it. She didn't have a choice. Luke didn't share her affections, not in the same way.

Her cell chimed as she climbed out of her car. Kelsey's text lit up the screen. Welcome home party planned. Cake ordered. Can't wait to C U.

Ditto, she typed and hit Send. *See all the good that lay ahead?* Her life awaited her in sunny Malibu. Wasn't that great? Wasn't that fab? Wasn't that what she'd been waiting for?

But as much as she loved her friends, she didn't miss them like she once had.

Her text chimed as she crossed the lot. This time it was from Colbie. Just picked up the cake. Mom & I R on R way!

Great. She answered, her heart heavy. She'd made friends here, ones she didn't want to leave. Should Lil B coming?

She needs out of the house. No worries.

Okay, at least she could stop worrying about Lil. She breezed into the small country grocery store, trying to orient herself. Where were the chips?

"Honor." Luke's brother was one aisle away putting things in a cart. "Keep going. You'll find him two rows down."

"Thanks, Hunter." She barely had time to prepare herself before she glimpsed Luke holding two bags of tortilla chips in each hand, clearly debating. His head was bent, his face tucked into a thoughtful frown. Wishes rose up, wishes for her future with him, wishes she had to ignore.

"Get them both." She squared her shoulders, determined to do this the right way. "How could you go wrong with extra nacho *and* spicy jalapeño?"

"You just can't." He lowered both bags into his rather full shopping cart. "I'd've been puzzling over that choice for a long time if you hadn't come along."

"Right. Like that was likely. Looks like you've been busy."

"Didn't realize I was so low on party supplies." He pulled a bag of pretzels off the rack. "This is an important get-together. It's your last day in Montana and Lil's first day out since leaving the hospital."

"Colbie told me she was doing well considering." She joined Luke as he shoved the cart down the aisle, hating that sweet Lil had to go through this.

"She has a lot more challenges, but her spirits are high." Luke turned, arrowing his cart toward the refrigerated shelves. "It's hard to keep Lil down for long."

"I've noticed. Colbie has been keeping me informed."

"You and my sisters have become good friends."

"And we'll stay that way." A blessing she was deeply grateful for. "Brooke has already vowed to come see me on their stopover in L.A. come late August."

"That's right, their honeymoon cruise." Luke chose two tubs from the shelving. "French onion or ranch? Wait, I already know the answer."

"Then why did you ask it?" She chose a container of salsa and added it to the cart. Her fingers brushed his. *Just ignore the lightning zap,* she told herself and stepped away. "How about avocado dip?"

"Better get two tubs. You've never seen the twins and avocado dip."

"What about you?"

"All I can say is you'd better get another thing of salsa, too. That way there's some for the rest of you."

"The truth comes out. You are a salsa hog."

"Hey, I never said I wasn't."

It felt natural at Luke's side, as if she belonged here and always would. But that wasn't true. She had to stop and remind herself that she didn't belong here, not forever. Not in the way she wanted. So why did her imagination betray her by flashing impossible images in her head? Images of a future with him buying groceries in this little store, having fun little moments and sharing jokes as they decided on their purchases. In that image she cradled a baby in her arms while a toddler sat strapped into the cart's seat.

Dreams she wished could be.

By the time they'd turned their cart toward the registers, Hunter beat them to it. He drove his cart into line ahead of them at the only available checker. "Did you remember napkins?"

"Roger that." Luke swung into place behind his brother. "Did you get the right hamburger buns, not the cheap ones?"

"He's the bane of my existence." Hunter shot Honor a wink. "Is there any room in your car for me? Maybe I'd like to get away. Give California a chance."

"Right. You'd change your mind before you hit the state line." Luke shook his head. "Don't pay him any attention. He needs me."

"Need, yes. Like? That's debatable." Affection belied the man's words as he began unloading his purchases onto the counter.

"Uh oh." Luke leaned in to whisper in her ear. "See that woman ahead of Hunter in line?"

"The one counting out every penny?" It was hard to concentrate with him so close. His nearness made her heart ache, so it was tough to notice the thin woman counting out coupons to the cashier. A grade-school-aged boy with matching brown hair stood silently beside her

"That's Millie Wilson. She's Hunter's long-ago girl-friend. He hasn't noticed her yet." Luke looked pained, as if he didn't expect the reunion to go well. "I didn't know she was back in town."

"Will Hunter be okay?" She felt sorry for the man intently loading packages of hamburger buns onto the conveyer belt, unaware of impending heartache. That's what love did, it made you hope, it filled you with wishes and made you believe in things that never turned out. Things that were never meant to be.

Don't go down that road, she told herself, fisting her hands tightly. Falling for Luke? That had been her fault.

"I can't take this one. It's past date." The cashier handed a coupon back to Millie.

"Oh, I'm sorry." The woman's hand trembled as she took the square of paper.

"That makes your total $17.03."

The woman dug in her coin purse. Soft straight brown hair shielded her face, hiding most of her features. "Uh, can you take off the box of crackers?"

"Oh, for heaven's sake." Hunter flipped two dollars onto the conveyer belt in the cashier's direction. "Enid, take it. I'm not gonna wait while—"

He froze, maybe finally really looking at the woman ahead of him. His jaw dropped and he fell silent, leaving the rest of his thought unspoken.

"Hi, Millie." Luke broke the shocked silence. "How's your dad?"

"Holding his own, but it's bad." She turned toward them, lifting her chin with dignity as she handed the cashier the box of crackers, refusing Hunter's offer. "They caught it way too late to do anything."

"Word has gotten around. The whole congregation is praying for him."

"Thanks, Luke," she answered, counting out exact change and handing them to Enid. "If anyone needs prayers, it's my dad. It was nice seeing you."

She didn't glance at Hunter, who stood statue-still, staring at the woman who accepted the single bag of groceries and walked away.

Honor recognized broken hearts when she saw them. She lifted her chin, determined not to let her own heart-break show. This is what love got you. Hurt and devastation. Smart things to avoid.

"Hunter, move along, we're waiting." Luke nudged his brother. The automatic doors opened and closed, Millie and her child were out of the building but not out of sight of the long front windows. A rusty, thirty-year-old Ford waited for them. "Are you all right?"

Hunter cleared his throat, nodded and gave his cart a shove forward. His nod might say yes, but his slumped shoulders said something different.

Some loves a person never got over. She knew just how he felt.

He'd been numb through all this. That was how he'd coped, but the minute Luke spotted Honor's car in the parking lot, his numbness shattered as if from a bomb blast. Shards and splinters were all that remained of his defenses. Those suitcases stacked in her backseat pierced him to the core.

This was it. Today was all he got with her. When she drove away from his home tonight, it would be for good.

With the numbness gone, he didn't know how to deal. She sauntered over to her car, pulling out her keys and ignoring the chime of her cell phone. "It's probably Anna Louise. They're planning my welcome home party."

"Sounds nice." He cleared his throat, wishing his voice didn't sound raw, and plopped sacks of groceries from the cart onto the crew seat of his truck. "You're getting lots of cake these days."

"I know, right?" She propped open her door, swiping gossamer tendrils out of her eyes. Golden beauty, shining spirit, she was everything he wanted in life. But did she know it?

No. What would she think if she knew? Luke hefted the last bag into the truck and gave the cart a shove. It rattled neatly into the metal collector he'd parked next to. The way Sonya had laughed at him when he'd asked her to stay flashed into his mind, along with her words. *You think I'd choose you over Chicago?* He would never forget how breezy she'd been, lighthearted at the prospect of leaving rural Montana.

Just like someone else he knew.

Face it, you've got to stop falling for city girls. He squared his shoulders and headed straight for the blond beauty leaning against her car, thumbing a message into her phone. She had a full life back home. Her dream job waiting for her.

Life on a rural Montana ranch couldn't compete. He couldn't compete

"Just sending Anna Louise a text." She shoved her

phone into her pocket. "Beach picnic scheduled for Monday evening about five minutes after I make it home."

"Sounds like a good way to celebrate. You've been missing that ocean."

"Not as much as you think."

His heart caught, hoping she meant more, that the evening at the lake meant as much to her as it did to him, but her breezy smile belied those words. So light-hearted, happy at the prospect of returning home. His throat tightened up, making it hard to speak. "Probably having friends here has helped distract you from missing home."

"Probably."

"Glad we could get you that social time you were missing." Each word scraped painfully against his larynx. It cost him to keep his feelings tucked inside, where they were safe, where she would never have to know a small-town Montana cowboy had fallen hard for her. "Time flies when you're having fun."

"Fun. Yes, that's what we've been having." For an instant sadness shadowed her clear blue eyes.

Making him hope there was something there, that something had changed in her feelings for him, but she firmed her chin and it was gone in a flash. Hard to tell what that was.

Don't start hoping, he told himself. That was a sure way to get hurt. And not just hurt. Honor had the power to crush his heart like no woman ever had.

A dark truck rumbled to a stop. The window rolled down and Hunter scowled at him. "Get a move on. We're running behind."

"I'm coming." Luke wasn't fooled. He knew the exact meaning of the look Hunter shot him before motoring away. Hunter had been concerned from the start that no good could come of this. He hadn't been wrong. Already Luke's heart was breaking. Best not to make it any worse.

"You heard the man." He grabbed hold of Honor's open door and gestured inside. "Let's get this party started."

"I can't say no to that." She slipped into her front seat, as merry as a song. It was a happy day for her and he intended to do his best to keep it that way for her sake, no matter the cost to him.

Her happiness was all he wanted in life. He closed her door, trying to do the same to his heart. If he could close it up well enough, then he couldn't feel the devastation about to tear him apart.

Another thing she could say about the McKaslins: they knew how to throw a party. Excellent conversation, tons of laughter and great food. She'd lingered at the picnic table on Luke's back patio with the others. Only a few chocolate cake crumbs and a small blob of frosting remained on her plate. She didn't want the meal to end.

"I'm trying to explain to the customer," Bree said to her twin. "The monster muffins only come in one size. Monster size. And he said that no, it was because of the iced monster faces and could he please have a smaller one? And I said, no, the monster muffins only come in one size…"

"—Could not believe Oscar." Brooke leaned across the table, her hand in her husband's, her gaze bright with love. "What a good dog. He may have the sit and stay thing down, although I don't want to say it too soon as it might invite doom…"

"—maybe I really should get one of these." Mac,

Bree's fiancé, stole one of his teenaged brother's ear-buds and plugged it in. "It's cool you can watch TV shows on this thing…."

But it was Luke's rich baritone that caught her attention and held it. He and his brother were out on the lawn, wrestling the tetherball poles into place. "A little to your left, Hunter."

"You mean *your* left," the other man grumbled.

"That's what I meant. Your other left."

"Honor?" Colbie's voice came as if from far away, although she was only across the table. "It's got to be tough leaving, huh?"

"I never thought it would be." Why the truth came so easily when she was talking to Colbie, she didn't know. This was Luke's sister, the last person she should be confessing to. If Luke knew how she felt…no, she shook her head, remembering how he'd pulled away from her in the rain. How he didn't kiss her.

How he'd greeted her in the grocery store today like a good, old friend. How he'd said their time together had just been *fun*. She ignored the hitch of pain and reached for her glass of lemonade.

"We're going to miss you, I'll tell you that." Colbie patiently cut a small piece of cake and held it up for her mother. Lil's good hand rose up, her fingers curling around Colbie's and took the fork, managing fairly well left-handed. "We've gotten used to hanging with you."

"There's still email. We can stay in touch, right?"

"Absolutely. That's a promise." Colbie's gaze was kind as she took the empty fork from her mother's hand. "Do you want more, Mom?"

Lil managed to shake her head, silent when she'd once been so talkative.

"Okay, then we're done." Colbie pushed away from

the table. "You're looking tired, Mom. Let's get you lying down."

Lil shook her head, although she did look pale. Honor appreciated how hard it was to leave the festivities and the family. She rose from the bench, considered gathering up the plates but decided to give Colbie a hand, first. She ran ahead to open the door and held it as the wheelchair rolled by.

"Thanks," Colbie sang as she pushed her mom into the kitchen.

It had to be tough keeping up her spirits for her mother, but Colbie never seemed to fail. Honor went to close the door and her gaze arrowed straight to the back lawn and the wide-shouldered man wrestling with the net. His sandy hair tousled in the wind, his chiseled face gentled by humor and he froze, as if he felt her look on him like a touch. He turned, nodded when he spotted her in the doorway. For an instant he seemed forlorn, as if he'd lost his best friend in the world.

It was gone in the next breath, replaced by a sunny smile. "You're on my team," he called out. "Hope you brought something besides those sandals. I intend to win."

"Sorry." Pain hit so hard her knees went weak. She leaned against the doorframe for support. "You're gonna lose."

"That remains to be seen." His words carried on the wind, warm and wonderful, wrapping around her like a blessing. A blessing so sweet and welcome, she never wanted to let it go.

She let the screen door slap shut and wandered through the adorable cottage to the back bedroom. Luke's room. Neat and orderly, with plain white walls and a blue comforter. She helped Colbie transfer and settle Lil onto the bed, wondering how she would find the strength to leave when the time came.

It wasn't fair how you didn't actually have to be in a relationship to get a broken heart. Even when he didn't love you back, love was like walking through a mine field. It was only a matter of time before you were blown away, never to be whole again.

That's what would happen to her when this party ended and she had to say goodbye to Luke.

You're going to have to help me, Lord, she prayed, as she handed Colbie the blanket draped across the foot of the bed. No way could she do this on her own.

Chapter Sixteen

"Match point." Luke held up one hand and caught the ball, ignoring the catch in his chest. This was it. The game was almost over. He moved into line, ready to serve. "Whoever wins this, wins the match. Ready?"

"Bring it!" called Brooke, with her eye on the ball.

He fisted his hand, swung back and let it go. The ball swooped across the net, Honor leaped to hit it. Colbie rushed in and slammed it home. He watched the ball bounce off the grass, heard Liam's groan of frustration and that was it. The game was over.

"Victory!" Brooke's fist shot up in the air. "Too bad Hunter had to leave, though. Do you think we should see if he needs help?"

"He would have called." Before the game started, Milton from next door had asked for help with the milking. Hunter had left, looking glad to get out of the game. His big brother had been off ever since seeing Millie in the grocery store. Luke had an inkling how Hunter might be feeling. A shattered heart affected a man. It was as simple as that.

"At least I'm going out as a victor." Honor headed his way. "Too bad you can't say the same."

"I always seem to be on the losing side." He stopped to pet Betty, who stood at the fence line, leaning against it, curiously watching the family's festivities. "That's why I invited you to Brooke's wedding in the first place. You were supposed to be my ringer."

"Oops. Didn't work that way, did it?"

"No, but that wasn't the only reason I invited you."

"I know." She ducked her chin, as if self-conscious, a little gesture that got to him.

How he was going to say goodbye, he didn't know. He couldn't stop picturing her here in his life, filling his kitchen with her laughter, his life with her humor and his heart with her sunshine. She wasn't his future, but a future with her was all he could see. Birthdays, holidays, quiet evenings sitting side by side reading on the front porch together. Children, anniversaries, growing old together. All of it sounded like the most perfect of all blessings.

There was no chance for any of it. Best just to let those dreams go.

"You're going to leave now, aren't you?" He leaned against the wooden fence post, trying to act casual and strong.

"You know I am. I booked a hotel in Bozeman. I'd like to get there before dark."

"I thought you were going to stay with the twins tonight?"

"They offered, but as I'm getting up with the sun to get a good day's drive in, I didn't want to wake them at four in the morning."

"And on a Saturday morning. Guess I'd better walk you to your car."

"I'd like that. Let me say goodbye to everyone first."

She left him behind, taking off for the picnic table where Colbie was pouring lemonade for everyone.

"Look who we have here. The California girl getting ready to leave." Colbie handed her a plastic cup. "You can take this to go if you want."

"Not that we want you to go," Bree chimed in.

"We'd calf rope you and hobble you if it would make you stay," Brandi joked. "You'll promise to email?"

"I pinky swear." She hooked her little finger with Brandi's to seal the deal. Her chest hurt so badly with repressed emotion she could barely get her words out. "I'll be lonely if you all don't stay in touch with me."

"We feel the same way," Brooke assured her, moving in to hug her next. Bree and Colbie came next to say their goodbyes. She had to blink hard to keep her vision clear.

"Give my love to Lil." She polished off her lemonade, set her cup on the table and gathered up her bag and keys. Her feet didn't want to carry her forward because her heart held her back. The tie she felt to the Mc-Kaslins, and more strongly to Luke, kept her in place, refusing to let her go.

You have to do it, she told herself, digging deep for the strength. The Lord must have helped her because she didn't know how her shaky legs carried her all the way to her car. Or how she managed to face the man who followed her there, his shadow falling over her with the sun at his back.

"Guess this is it." His face in shadow was a mystery to her, a dark mask she couldn't read.

"Guess so." She popped the trunk and tossed her gym bag in. "Thanks for the party. It was a fun way to end my time here."

"It was my pleasure." He bowed his head, his face

even harder to read. "You have a safe drive. When you stop for the night, maybe you could send an email."

"Maybe." She reached for her car door but he beat her to it. He towered over her, made larger than life by the endless blue sky framing him.

And by her feelings for him, so great they had no limit.

Please say you feel that way, too. She waited for him to stop her, but he didn't. He stood patiently holding her door, the friend he'd intended to be all along. Clutching her keys, she slipped into the sun-hot seat. This was the last chance for him to stop her, but instead, he closed her door.

So, that's how he felt. She bowed her head, taking a moment to sort through her key ring and so she could gather her strength. She knew he cared. His kiss, his kindness and the way he treated her told her that. But it wasn't enough. She swallowed hard, slipped on her sunglasses to hide the tears swimming in her eyes and started the engine.

Your heart is not breaking, she told herself firmly. *This is not the end of the world.*

Except it did feel that way. She rolled down the window, praying the smile she put on her face fooled him. "No excuses this time. You finish the book before our next Good Books discussion. Every chapter. Got it?"

"Yes, ma'am. What about you? If you give orders, you'd best be able to take them. The discussion is tomorrow night. I've got time tonight and tomorrow to read."

"I have the audiobook." Her smile seemed falsely bright. "I have a whole day on the open road."

"That you do."

"Something tells me I'll be able to finish it in time."

"Then I'll see you in the chat room?"

"That's the plan." Her chin wobbled a bit, but the sunglasses hid her eyes from him. Her real feelings were a mystery.

What were the chances that this was killing her, too? He jammed his hands into his pockets and rocked back on his heels. What if he asked her to stay. Would she? Would she want a life in Montana with him? She had a good life in California.

"Do you have everything?" That's what he asked instead of risking his heart. "Another lemonade? A piece of cake for the hotel?"

"No, thanks. I'm good."

"Okay, then." Awkward, he stepped back from the car, saying nothing more because the rest of the McKaslins ambled into sight, grouped together, arm in arm.

"Text when you get there!" Colbie called out.

"So we know you made it—" Bree started.

"—safe and sound," Brandi finished.

"Can't wait to see you next month," Brooke chimed in. "We'll do lunch."

"I know just the place." Smiling like this was killing her as she put her car in gear. "Goodbye. Thanks for your friendship."

Goodbyes filled the air like a chorus. Only Luke stood apart, his granite face carved into a mask she couldn't read. He'd turned so the sun fell across him, illuminating him perfectly. Strong man.

Tender heart.

That got her every time.

He lifted one hand in farewell as she pulled away. He was an image in her rearview mirror as she rolled down the driveway, diminishing with distance. Soon he was nothing but a blur in the mirror and when she turned onto the country road, he was gone. She had to stop hoping he wanted her.

Sobs built in her throat, but she held them down. Tears blurred her vision but she blinked them away. Wasn't this why she hadn't wanted to get involved in the first place? Wasn't this why she'd only wanted to stay friends? To spare herself from this heartache.

She gripped the steering wheel tighter, adjusted the air conditioner and guided her car down the ribbon of road, heading straight into the sunset. The dream of Luke McKaslin had been a lot to lose.

"It's over, Betty." Luke stabbed the slab of alfalfa with the tines of his pitchfork. "Honor's gone."

The cow watched him with curious eyes, mooing her sympathy. He forked the alfalfa over the fence rail, doing his best to keep busy, to keep moving. Maybe if he didn't stop to feel it, loss wouldn't have a chance to sink in.

Except it wasn't working. He couldn't ignore the pain hitting him square in the chest. Heartbreak took a hold of him he couldn't break. He could still see her driving away, taking a piece of him with her.

Why hadn't he taken the risk when he'd had the chance? If he'd spotted a hint of vulnerability in her eyes or read the slightest wish on her face, he'd have done it. If he thought for one instant that she felt like this for him, he'd have been down on his knee, asking her to love him.

Betty nudged him with her nose, interrupting his thoughts.

"She has everything she wants back home in California. Why would she stay? But I should have asked. Now I'll always wonder what if." He rubbed the cow's nose, grateful for her sympathetic company. "To be honest, I didn't think it would hurt this much to watch her go."

"Typical man thinking." The grass crackled behind him as Brooke trekked closer. "Why is it so difficult for you men to follow your hearts?"

"Because we try not to feel them."

"Finally. A little honesty." Brooke shook her head, scattering her dark hair. "What is your heart telling you about Honor?"

"That I'd made a mistake when I kissed her."

"You kissed her? When?"

"It doesn't matter now." That had been before her dream job. When he'd thought he had a chance to win her. Kissing her had been the wrong move, he could see now. If he hadn't kissed her, then maybe he could be convincing himself right now that he wasn't dying inside.

Betty batted her eyes at Brooke and leaned over the top fence rail, begging for attention. Brooke obliged, rubbing the cow's forehead.

It was a lovely night. Soft sunlight, the sheen of color lighting the underbellies of the clouds and the promise of impending sunset gave the evening a peaceful air. But he couldn't feel it. Every moment that passed, he hurt worse. Like a vise clamping down on his sternum that refused to stop.

"Luke, are you okay?" Brooke squeezed his arm, concerned. "You don't look all right."

"I'm fine." The words came clipped and abrupt, but it was the best he could do. He couldn't forget the image of Honor driving away. He kept seeing it over and over in Technicolor glory, digging more deeply every time, making a deeper wound.

No, he had no idea losing her would hurt like this.

He'd been through heartbreak before. Never had it felt like this.

"Let me guess how you're feeling." Brooke leaned against the fence rails, gazing out at the peaceful valley. "It's like you'll never get a proper breath again because of the terrible hole in your chest."

"That would be accurate." He couldn't deny it. And the hole kept getting bigger.

"Every rib feels as if it's been broken twelve times."

"Maybe thirteen."

"You feel like the sun has set and will never rise again."

"Something like that." It was hard to admit Honor meant that much to him, because it was tough being this vulnerable. Harder still to let down the guards around his heart and feel what was there. Especially when he'd tried so hard all along not to.

"You feel like you've lost a big part of yourself and you'll never get it back." Brooke picked a daisy from the wild grasses at their feet.

"Yeah." He swallowed hard, wishing he didn't have to acknowledge the place in him that felt empty, the piece Honor took.

"Do you know what that means?" Brooke plucked one daisy petal and let it fall on the wind.

"Yes, but I don't want to admit it."

"Oh, you big tough guys. I think you fall harder than any others." Brooke picked off another petal. "You love her. You love her not."

"Sure, I was a little sweet on Honor, but—"

"You love her." Brooke sent another petal fluttering on the wind. "You love her not."

"Okay, fine." Saying the words wouldn't change anything, but they finally rolled off his tongue. "I love her. Really love her. I didn't want to let her go."

"There. Was that so hard to admit?"

"It was." He rubbed the spot on his chest, hurting bad enough to bring him to his knees. Not that he intended to show it.

"Then go get her, big brother." Brooke's smile turned mischievous. "I happen to know where she's staying."

Chapter Seventeen

The last, bright rays of sunset lit the hotel's parking lot with a crimson glow as she trundled her suitcase along the sidewalk. Her feet felt heavy, but not as heavy as her heart.

You can do this, Honor. Keep going forward. Don't look back. Whatever you do, don't think of him.

But it was impossible. Love, deeper than she'd realized, lived in her heart. Stubborn. Impossible to stop. What was she going to do about it?

She didn't know. It wasn't like she could drive back to Luke's place and declare her love. She squinted at the row of doors, found room 134 and headed toward it. She blinked, but she kept remembering Luke's image in her rearview mirror growing smaller, looking forlorn and lost, his head bowed as she'd driven away.

I would have stayed for him, she told the Lord as she stopped in front of her door. *I would have loved it here in Montana.*

She hadn't realized it, but this place had become home. She already missed the warmth of the McKaslin camaraderie, the view of the mountains from Luke's place and Betty. She hadn't said goodbye to Betty.

Her cell chimed, startling her out of her reveries. She inserted the keycard in the slot and the lock beeped open. She hauled in her suitcase, tossed her bag on the neatly made bed and drew open the curtains. The view of the parking lot was stunning.

Fine, that was sarcasm. But she really did miss trees and meadows and shimmering purple mountains. Imagine that.

This isn't helping, she realized, as more grief crashed over her. It just kept coming. What she needed was distraction, and the best way to do that was to see who'd texted her. The text she'd received was probably from Kelsey, who'd threatened to check up on her this evening, wanting updates so she could adjust the time of the welcome home party accordingly.

Determined to push any thoughts of Luke from her mind, she plopped into the armchair by the window. She reached for her phone, but Luke's number stared back at her. Not Kelsey's.

Did she open it? Or would it be easier on her heart to just let it go?

Her phone chimed with a second text message. From Luke. She squeezed her eyes shut. Could she do it? Could she keep being friends with him, or would it always hurt this much?

Her phone chimed a third time. Feeling God's hand on her shoulder, knowing she didn't have to do this alone, her thumb hit the key that brought up his message. Two words lit up her screen.

I'm sorry.

For what? she typed and hit Send. Luke had always been wonderful, a perfect gentleman. He'd been an awe-

some…friend wasn't the right word. He was more than
that. He would *always* be more than that. Nothing she
could do could change that. Her heart had decided on
him.

His answer flashed onto her screen. For letting you
go tonight.

She had to swipe her eyes before she could text him
back. Well, I had 2 get on the road. I have a driving
schedule 2 keep.

Forget the driving schedule.

Of course she needed a schedule. But I planned it
carefully.

U know what they say. Plans R meant 2 B broken.

Where was he going with this? She couldn't see it.
Too much had happened today for her to think clearly.
She swiped her eyes again, wishing those pesky tears
would stop, but they just kept coming. Talking to him
like this—as friends—was agony. She couldn't do it
anymore.

Her phone chimed. Look out UR window.

She squinted at the message. Now he really wasn't
making any sense. She looked up and a man's blurred
shape crossed the parking lot, walking in her direction.
Not that she could see very clearly, but she'd know that
shade of sandy hair anywhere. Only one man she knew
had those strong shoulders and easy-going gait.

Luke! She grabbed hold of the doorframe without
remembering getting up from the chair or crossing the
room. What was he doing here? Why couldn't she do a
better job at hiding her joy at seeing him again?

Her cell phone chimed with one final text.

I love U.

She stared at the screen, the words blurring until she couldn't read them.

"I sure hope you feel the same way." He towered over her, her very own Montana cowboy, saying the words she longed to hear.

"You love me?" She couldn't believe it. Was she dreaming? Was this really true?

"I love you so much, darlin', I can't live without you. I know this for sure."

Words brought more tears to her eyes. This was real. She laid her hand on his chest, feeling how real he was. "You really love me?"

"More than words can say. I'll sell out my half of the dairy to Hunter if I have to. I'll learn to surf. I'll take up beachcombing. I'll do whatever I have to, if only you think one day you can come to love me, too."

"No, I'm sorry. That's not going to happen."

"You mean you don't want me?" Pain shone in his eyes.

The poor man. He really didn't get it, did he? Had she protected her heart that much? So that he couldn't even guess her true feelings at all?

"No," she corrected him, tenderly, letting her affection show in her voice. "I can't come to love you, because I already do. I love you, Luke McKaslin."

"You don't know how glad I am to hear that." Joy rumbled in his words as he opened his arms to her. "I need you so much, Honor. Don't think I can breathe without you."

"I know just how you feel." She stepped into the

strong arms of the man she adored beyond all else. Her one true love. Once she was tucked against his chest, she felt whole. Her world felt right. She had found her home.

And it was him.

She tipped back her head to peer up at him. "Are you sure you want to become a California guy?"

"I can do it." Those dimples of his could make a girl swoon. "I might have to leave Betty behind, though."

"Yes, as I'm fairly sure they don't allow cows on the beach." She held on to him so tight, she was never going to let him go. "As I've grown fairly fond of Betty, too, maybe we should just stay here."

"In Montana? You would do that? What about your job?"

"What's a job compared to a life spent here with you?" She felt his heart skip a beat and when he leaned in to kiss her, she'd never known such bliss. His kiss spoke of fairy-tale wishes and storybook happiness and promises made to be kept.

This was true love's kiss.

Epilogue

One week later

Honor's cell chimed, although she could barely hear it above the rush of the waves slapping the shore. The constant music of the ocean wasn't so different from the wind in a forest, she decided. Different, but also wondrous.

"I can't believe you are packing up and leaving me." Kelsey gave her long black hair a toss. "Not that I can blame you. Look at that man. Amazing."

"He really is." She stopped to let the water wash over her bare toes, keeping one eye on the man up ahead, talking with Anna Louise's fiancé.

Luke had blown her away as a Montana cowboy, but standing on the beach in a white T-shirt and denim cutoffs, he looked right at home. As always, her heart gave a little swoop.

"You totally love him. Oh, I know just how you feel." Anna Louise gave a dramatic sigh, her engagement ring sparkling in the sun. "Do you think he's going to propose soon?"

"No idea, but we've talked about getting married one day."

While her friends squealed in delight at the prospect of another wedding, she decided to check her messages. Just one, from Jerrod Lambert.

I aced it, no problem, he'd written. Thanks, Teach.

Wow. He'd done well, just as she knew he would. She'd answer him later, when she didn't have her friends seizing her by the arms.

"C'mon. It's time for our dinner reservation." Kelsey tugged her along.

"This is our last big celebration together." Anna Louise trudged ahead, bouncing with happiness. "At least until my wedding."

"Not that we won't text like crazy," Honor pointed out.

"And talk on the phone," Kelsey added.

"And we can always fly the friendly skies when we can't take being part another minute." Anna Louise rushed ahead. Tom, the piano tuner, gave her a besotted look. "Hey, handsome. Wanna take me to dinner?"

"Gladly." Tom offered Anna Louise his arm. Kelsey hurried to join them as they headed toward the restaurant on the pier. Which meant she was alone with Luke, with her beloved.

"This is pretty great." He held out his hand to her. "Are you sure you don't want to live in California? My offer still stands. I can move out here. This ocean view isn't so bad."

"We can always come visit, how about that?" She loved the feel of her hand in his, their fingers together. "But from now on, I'm always going to be a Montana girl."

"Always. I like the sound of that." He strode beside

her, adjusting his gait to match hers. Tomorrow bright and early they would head home with her possessions packed into a little moving truck. Already Luke's sisters had found her an apartment not far from Colbie's home, and she'd even applied for a job at the Prospect school district. It would all work out, she knew, because their future was safe in God's hands.

"I think it's only fair to warn you, Honor."

"Warn me about what?"

"It looks like we're heading for a happy ending." He pulled her into his arms.

"Yes, we are. It's going to be the happiest ever."

His kiss was proof of that. Infinitely tender. Flawless. The perfect start to their happy ending. As if heaven agreed, the sunshine brightened like a blessing, casting them in pure gold.

Yes, a definite happy ending.

* * * * *

Dear Reader,

The McKaslin Clan stories are like coming home for me. When you pick up this book, I hope you feel the same way. I've had Luke's story in mind for many years, just waiting to be told, a tale about two people who meet online at a book reader's site and strike up a friendship. Luke is hoping for more, although Honor is in no way ready for another relationship. Of course, the minute you make plans in life, they are bound to change. I hope you enjoy this tender love story of two deserving hearts.

Thank you for choosing *Montana Cowboy* and for returning to the McKaslin family with me.

As always, wishing you love and peace,

Jillian Hart

Questions for Discussion

1. What are your first impressions of Luke? How would you describe him?

2. What are your first impressions of Honor? What do you learn about her from the way she handles Jerrod? Treats her friends? What does this tell you about her character?

3. Why do you think Luke has developed a crush on Honor, even when their only contact has been over the computer? Have you ever had this happen to you?

4. Why isn't Honor a Montana girl at the beginning of the book? What influences her? How does this change?

5. What do you think Honor expects when she first meets Luke face-to-face? How does meeting Luke and his family change her?

6. Why do you think Luke is so shy about sharing his feelings? What is at the core of this?

7. Family and friends speculate and meddle in Honor and Luke's relationship. What part do they play in the budding romance? How does this affect Honor? Luke?

8. What makes Honor begin to fall for Luke? When do you think she really falls in love with him?

9. What are Luke's strengths? What are his weaknesses? What do you come to admire about him?

10. What values do you think are important in this book?

11. What do you think are the central themes in this book? How do they develop? What meanings do you find in them?

12. How does God guide both Honor and Luke? How is this evident? How does God lead them to true love?

13. There are many different kinds of love in this book. What are they? What do Honor and Luke each learn about true love?

—TEXAS TWINS—

Follow the adventures of two sets of twins who are torn apart by family secrets and learn to find their way home.

Her Surprise Sister by Marta Perry
July 2012

Mirror Image Bride by Barbara McMahon
August 2012

Carbon Copy Cowboy by Arlene James
September 2012

Look-Alike Lawman by Glynna Kaye
October 2012

The Soldier's Newfound Family
by Kathryn Springer
November 2012

Reunited for the Holidays
by Jillian Hart
December 2012

Available wherever
books are sold.

www.LoveInspiredBooks.com

LICONT0812

celebrating 15 YEARS *Love Inspired*

A story of inspiration, family
and blossoming love from author

Barbara McMahon

In tiny Grasslands, Texas, Maddie Wallace has discovered
she has a family she hadn't known existed—including an
identical twin sister, who is vastly different. When ranch
foreman and single father Ty Garland hires her as the
nanny for the daughter *he* has just discovered, the two
learn they have more in common than imagined. But is
Grasslands the place where Maddie truly belongs…in
every single way?

Mirror Image Bride

—TEXAS TWINS—

www.LoveInspiredBooks.com

LI87758R